# The Erotic Notebooks

YASMINE MILLETT

Copyright © 2023 T.M Cicinski
All rights reserved.
ISBN: 9798372421158
Cover Photograph By Grantas Vaičiulėnas

# THE STORIES

... Prologue
... A Glimpse of Life on the Other Side
... A First Experiment With Exhibitionism
... A Second Experiment With Exhibitionism
... The Surprises and Pleasures of a Country Night
... The Cinematic Evening
... The Interview
... A Rare and Beautiful Rose
... The Pianist
... Mad as Birds
... What It was Like For Him
... The Quiet Woman
... Across a Narrow Street
... The Gentleman, Part One
... The Gentleman, Part Two
... The Artist's Assistant
... A Night For Strangers
... Epilogue

"You'll regret only the lovers you didn't have."
— Emmanuelle Arsan, Emmanuelle

"You live like this, sheltered, in a delicate world, and you believe you are living. Then you read a book…. Or you take a trip… and you discover that you are not living, that you are hibernating. The symptoms of hibernating are easily detectable: first, restlessness. The second symptom (when hibernating becomes dangerous and might degenerate into death): absence of pleasure. That is all. It appears like an innocuous illness. Monotony, boredom, death. Millions live like this (or die like this) without knowing it. They work in offices. They drive a car. They picnic with their families. They raise children. And then some shock treatment takes place, a person, a book, a song, and it awakens them and saves them from death. Some never awaken."
— Anaïs Nin, The Diary, Volume 1.

# PROLOGUE

This book came about as the result of a single conversation. It was never meant of course to be a book, and its contents have been edited slightly from what they were before it was one. Certain names have been changed for example, perhaps even our own, and the order and introductions of the stories has been altered in a few small ways I will not go into. Nonetheless, every word contained within is a product of that one conversation, which took place when Dominic and I had known each other barely three weeks. Appropriately, given what you will go on to read, we had that conversation lying in bed one summer's afternoon with the clean, bright sunlight streaming in upon us through the chinks in the shutters.

I was drowsy in that moment, but not with the drowsiness of tiredness; drowsy with a perfect satisfaction of the body that came from the warmth of the day, and from the distant sound of the sea and of a light breeze rustling through the branches outside of the window of the hotel room; from the memory of Dominic's kisses, his touch, still fresh on my body, the faint throbbing ache of pleasure that lingered still between my thighs, and from the fact of his body touching lightly against mine.

Slowly, lazily, I rolled over onto my side to look at him, and I remember seeing his deeply tanned, handsome face looking thoughtful, with his beautifully haunting eyes gazing blankly up at the ceiling. I found the look on his face faintly troubling. It seemed so at odds with the satisfaction I felt in that moment.

"What are you thinking?" I asked him, softly, half-anxious to hear his reply, but half-too-satisfied to worry. My days of worrying too much about the unknown, about things I could only guess at or wait to pass were in the past, I hoped. Through many struggles, I had taught myself not to worry;

not to let anxiety gnaw at me; to live and let what had to be, or what might be, simply be.

He glanced at me and smiled that subtle, faintly wicked smile of his before returning his gaze to the ceiling.

"I was just thinking about making love to you," he said. The directness of the answer took me a little aback, as truly direct answers always do. So few people are genuinely sincere. Most people hide their sentiments, their desires, their thoughts, behind veiled phrases, behind indirectness. When someone feels no need to do so, there is always something refreshing about it and a little frightening. This was the case with him. There was no hesitancy then in his voice, only a thoughtfulness. "I was wondering," he went on, "whether I satisfy you. Not superficially, but deeply; as you dream of being satisfied."

I kept looking at him, focussing on those eyes, wondering whether they would tell me those things that his words did not. For my part, I realised then that I did not know if I satisfied him either, in the way he described. I knew that I gave him pleasure, as he gave me pleasure. Yet I did not know if it was the type of pleasure he craved; if I fulfilled not just his physical need to make love, but his fantasies, his deeper desires; if I made love to him in the way that he would choose, could he have chosen any way he wanted. I did not know either, whether our lovemaking was that type of fleeting connection that satisfies the desires of the moment and then is moved on from, either to become subservient to love, less frequent, less necessary, as it becomes in many relationships, no more than a pleasant addition to something greater; or, as in the absence of love, to simply be left in the past, as a memory, while other lovers are sought to bring a more profound satisfaction. I had not thought about it until then. I had not, if truth be told, thought to wonder whether indeed a single lover might ever bring a full, rounded, complete satisfaction of all I had craved for a long time past, and that I imagined all lovers must crave. I thought of fleeting satisfaction, of happiness, of romance, of perfect silver screen moments shared with a companion, and of perfect blue movie moments too. Yet I never stopped to wonder whether that one companion might satisfy me completely, having assumed always that there would be another to follow who would touch a different chord in me, who would bring me a different pleasure, and that with all of them taken together I would create for myself a mosaic of experiences that gave me everything I wanted to experience in the course of my life; everything I wanted to feel, to enjoy. I liked, at least to begin with, the excitement of each new form of satisfaction – the unforeseeable nature of it; the not knowing which rich sensations, which fantasies, each new lover might allow me to fulfil. Yet I had never thought to tell anyone what it was that I *wanted*, to inspire them to fulfil my needs and desires consciously, consistently, and thus to make me want to remain with them knowing that they could give me everything that I wanted. To remain with a lover permanently, or at least for any significant period of time, had always seemed to me so limiting, so much like putting up a door, albeit a beautiful, elaborately carven door, between myself and the dark, mysterious entrance to the unknown, the unseen, the unexperienced; a door that closed those things off to me. It gave happiness, in my experience, to remain with a lover over some weeks or months, to explore them, to become comfortable with them, to express myself to the fullest extent that I thought they would accept. Over too long a period, however, I always found myself beginning to yearn for those things I was not receiving; those other forms of happiness that loyalty to one person caused to become inaccessible – to be glimpsed from afar yet always untasted, untouched, unfelt. It had never occurred to me, I realised then, to demand from any one lover explicitly all of those things for which my mind and body yearned. They might have not been willing, or happy, to give them to me, after all.

"I pass from one love to another," he said, seeming almost to steal the thoughts from my mind, "enjoying the newness first of our love-making and then those parts of my desires that my lover fulfils, sometimes even enjoying those things that I had never thought to desire. And equally I feel myself to be fulfilling some aspect of their desires, their physical wants, and their imaginings. Yet, always in the end, when the honeymoon of love has passed, since I shy away from asking the nature of those pleasures that I had not thought to give them, or from telling explicitly what I desire, what I enjoy, I am left, at least in part, unsatisfied, and haunted by the feeling that they feel the same. And so I leave, or they leave, and another lover comes to take their place, with whom I shall act in the same way. Between us, if I could have any wish, it would be to try something entirely different; to be honest in my desires, and to know yours, and to fulfil them; for you to be the first person I felt I had completely satisfied, body and imagination together, for whom there was no secret want left unfulfilled." He glanced back at me and his eyes met mine with an intensity, a powerful earnestness to them. "Tell me, Yasmine, honestly, without holding back, how do you feel? How satisfied are you when we are together?"

"I think I might feel the same as you feel," I said, surprising myself with my response since I had rarely thought myself to feel the same about such things as anyone. I had always felt my feelings and instincts and desires to be somewhat apart from those of the madding crowd. "For now, you satisfy me," I told him, truthfully. "I love to make love to you. Yet the thought of how it might be to be with a lover who knew me, who glimpsed all of the desires that lie within me, even the darkest ones, and accepted them and wanted to fulfil them, is something I have never allowed myself to imagine. And to know, truly know all that my lover wanted, and to feel that I gave it to them. There is something wonderful, and dangerous, and powerful, and exciting in that. Perhaps even that is the way to make the excitement endure, not fade a little more with every sunrise. Yet at the same time, I think I would be too afraid to ask; too afraid of my reaction on hearing, and too afraid to tell and see what reaction my lover might show. Though I might promise to tell all, I would not be honest. When I looked into their eyes, lies would come more naturally; to protect them, and me."

He shrugged.

"I suppose I would be the same in the end. As much as I want to know, what images or fantasies run through your mind when we make love; about your experiences in the past – what gave you most pleasure, what you would most wish to repeat, what your deepest desires might be, and how I might help you fulfil them – I am too shy to ask. And if I were not, I still would not know the right questions. But since we feel the same way, the question really should be is there anything we can do to surmount our instincts and fears and at least try to be open?"

I looked up at him then, at his handsome, thoughtful face, and at his eyes which were of such a strange, dark blue, and which I always felt were in danger hypnotising me with their mysterious depth. His lean, athletic body, with its strong arms and flat stomach that he should not still have possessed given his age and lifestyle, was warm against me, and I pressed my own against it, in part to reassure him, in part to reassure myself.

"Perhaps there is something we can do," I said at last. "You do not want to ask me, and neither do I you, but that does not have to prevent us telling one another. You are a writer, Dominic. And so am I. Why do we not simply write our experiences, or desires, our fantasies and most passionate, memorable moments each in a notebook and then exchange those notebooks so that we can read what we are afraid to hear; write what we are afraid to tell. And then we will know something at least of that aspect of one another. We will know if we are compatible. We will know what the other person dreams of, and we can decide whether or not we want to fulfil those desires."

He turned from his contemplation of the ceiling once more and looked at me intently.

"Would you not be shy to do so? To write explicitly what you have done, and what you want?"

I remember I thought about that and shook my head.

"It does not need to be explicit in that sense. We can write stories, true stories, or true fantasies, but containing only that which comes from us, not that which we want to be heard, and from them we will each be able to see patterns of desire, of fantasy, and we will each know the other person on a level that otherwise we might never know."

He slowly nodded his head, and smiled again that wicked smile from which the preoccupation had disappeared, replaced by something else; amusement perhaps, or excitement.

"Alright," he agreed. "When we finally get out of bed, we will buy the notebooks and begin…"

And so we did as we had agreed. The stories that follow are those I wrote for him. Why his stories do not appear alongside mine, I will tell later. Yet perhaps before I do, you will already have guessed.

# A GLIMPSE OF LIFE ON THE OTHER SIDE

The boyfriend I had when I first moved away from home and into a place of my own was the first person to make me realise that I was different from other people. That my desires were not others' desires. That my actions were not others' actions. That something in my nature made me think things, do things, want things that would never have occurred to other people. Or that, had they occurred to other people, those people would never have acted upon in the way that I acted upon them and afterwards taken such delight in them. For a long time the realisation made me feel separate from those around me; almost alone. It was only later that I came to realise that I was far from alone; that there existed in fact a small group of people, people hidden amongst the crowds, people in the shadowy corners of bars, people lying out on the beaches, laughing in the streets, who were just like me. The simple truth was that they were hard to distinguish from everyone else, just as I imagine I am hard to distinguish from those from whom I am secretly so different. At that time, however, I knew nothing of that small group. I knew only that my boyfriend was everything that everyone is supposed to want in a man. He was handsome. He had a beautiful body, which he knew how to use to bring me pleasure. He was intelligent and he respected me, and showed his respect for me in his every action and word. He was considerate; he never caused me to feel used or taken for granted or uncomfortable or jealous. He did not lie to me. He did not watch other women in the street with a gleam in his eyes that would have enabled me to see that he was imagining all the things he would like to do with them. Most of all, there was nothing he would not do for me. From the smallest favour, to the greatest sacrifice, I had but to ask, or even to indicate that I needed or desired something from him, and he would do it instantly. He was perfect and I knew I was a fool not to be head-over-heels in love to him, devoted to him, desperate to pass the rest of my life with him, but within a few months I was already tired of him. There was something missing, it seemed to me; something dark that he did not possess. I wanted sometimes for him to see me not as some angelic princess to be cared for and worshipped, but as an object to be used and cast aside. I wanted him to get angry, to tell me when I was tiresome. Yet he would not. I wanted him to want things that I would not give him, and thus to be dissatisfied. I wanted him to be passionate to the point of madness. I wanted to discover dark secrets about him that would drive me wild with anger and jealousy. Yet all of these things were beyond him. He had been so perfectly trained by society, by his family, by his own good nature, that he was patient with me where he should have been enraged, was respectful where I wanted him to be indomitable, and was thoughtful where I wanted a man simply to know what he wanted and to take it. His perfection made me feel dirty. I had all of those traits, which society calls flaws, that he lacked. I did not leave him then because I was waiting for myself to change, to mature into the type of person I felt I should have been, thinking that maybe that person might forever regret it if I left him. Also, I could not think of a way to explain to him why I did not love him. Yet, though I did not leave him, I began, unconsciously at first, then almost intentionally to take advantage of him. I allowed myself to get angry with him because I needed an outlet for my anger and he demonstrated so clearly that he would accept it placidly. I lied to him because I knew it was in his nature to believe me. I put him in uncomfortable positions because I knew he would not blame me for it. And I flirted with other men while he was beside me, desperate to see if there was a limit to his patience, and found to my despair that there seemed to be none. Sometimes I felt bad afterwards. Other times the memory of my cruelty served as a tonic that soothed my own feelings of failure, of inadequacy. Yet in that moment, despite my behaviour toward that example of society's perfect man, I still saw myself as not so different to others. I assumed they were like me. What opened my eyes finally to my difference from the majority and allowed me to see myself as I truly was, however, he did only accidentally.

One day, I made him come to my flat and put shelves up on the wall of my bedroom. He had had other commitments, but he had come, as any knight in shining armour would come, and had done what I had asked and only then had rushed off to do those things he had meant before to do. In rushing off, however, he had left the tools he had used in my hall, apologising for doing so, and promising to come back to collect them the next day so that they would not be in my way. Inadvertently, it was those tools that were to open my eyes, or that were more accurately to enable me to open my own eyes.

The building in which I had rented the flat in which I lived was an old three story town house, each floor of which had been divided into two flats, one small and comfortable like mine, the other large and luxurious. On my floor, the other tenant was man of means, though I did not know what he did. Perhaps he was a banker, or a property developer. Or perhaps he was a man of independent wealth. Whatever he did, it enabled him to dress exquisitely, to order champagne by the case, and to receive near weekly deliveries of art, carried to his door by men dressed in spotless overalls who greeted him in respectful, almost awed, tones. I knew all this from watching him through my peep hole when sometimes I heard voices, or a noise, outside my door and went to see what was passing. I had found almost immediately on moving there that I liked the feeling spying into the lives of others while they remained ignorant of my presence. I liked to hear, muffled yet nonetheless partially distinct through the door, the things they said when they thought that no-one other than their companion could hear. I liked to see them examine themselves in the long, gilt framed mirror at the end of the hall and imagine what they were thinking. I liked to see how they moved when they thought that no-one was watching, and to think then that I was seeing them as no-one else was seeing them. I would have liked to spy on my boyfriend the same way, but I could not see how to do so. This spying of course, I told myself, was not malicious, or something shameful, it was merely a manifestation of the curiosity that everyone felt. I was not alone in it. Sometimes, however, I wondered if I took it further than other people did; whether there were something disreputable in my persistence in intentionally watching others, rather than accidentally catching glimpses of them and watching from interest though knowing all the while that it was wrong. I did not, however, torment myself too long with worries about that. Through watching, I learned one other thing that my neighbour's money allowed him to do that I would not have missed for the world; something that made me more interested in him than I otherwise would have been – interested almost to the point of obsession. At least once a week, often more than once, he would come home late in the evening with the most beautiful, the most elegant, the most expensively dressed prostitutes on his arm. Escorts, they probably called themselves. Or companions. Or perhaps they had other names for themselves. Yet however they should have been labelled, it added up to the same thing. They were prostitutes, but of a class so rare and expensive that few would ever have been able to buy their favours. Sometimes he would pause with them in the hall and talk to them, or kiss them, or have them touch him through his clothes, or order them to undo their dresses so that he could kiss and fondle their breasts, all while I watched through the peep hole, hidden behind my door. He seemed to me as I watched him, so magnificently shameless. In those brief moments before his door closed behind him, he acted on his desires without hesitation. Whenever he said what he wanted, it took the form of a command. The simple fact that he said what he wanted, not what he expected the women to want to hear, was extraordinary to me, and thrilling. He ordered. He took. And either the women were wonderful actresses or, from the very beginning, they wanted it just as he did. Those women were extraordinary too. They seemed to revel in the situation in which they had placed themselves. They performed. They delighted. They were magnificent in a way that I had never felt myself to be. Oh, what pleasure I would have felt to be like them! At night sometimes, when I was alone or with my boyfriend, I would think of them, of how it would be to be in their positions, of how it would be to be as they were, and grow excited. I wanted, from the first moment of seeing them, to see more, to see what went on in my neighbour's flat after the door had shut, but of course there no way of doing so.

Then, when my boyfriend had been putting up the shelves for me, he had in all innocence made it seem less impossible. He had been drilling holes to put in the screws for the brackets that would support the shelves, and had stopped suddenly and pulled back. When I asked him what was wrong, he had told me that the wall in that part of the room above my bed seemed to be very thin, much thinner than in any other part; so thin in fact that he had almost drilled straight through into my neighbour's flat, into what must have been his living room. He had seemed very shaken by the idea and when he had finally gone back to work, I noticed that he was much more careful in that part of the wall, almost tentative. For myself too, I found myself shaken, but in an entirely different way. His words, that he might have put a hole straight through the wall, gave me the intoxicating idea that had he done so, I might have had a peep hole, not into the hall as with the one on my door, but into my neighbour's inner sanctum; that I might have been able to see what went on beyond, to catch a glimpse of the encounters that previously I had only ever been able to imagine. The thought made me almost breathless and sent shivers of fear and pleasure and shame running through me all at the same time.

After he left, I was tormented by the temptation to do just what he had avoided doing; to make a hole straight through the wall; a hole that would enable me to see what went on on the other side. No normal person would do such a thing, I told myself. It would be wrong. And besides, I might be caught. However, as the hours passed, and I imagined more and more intently what I might see, what scenes I might be able to live out vicariously, were I only to make that one small hole, that the chance of being caught seemed less of a deterrent. And that other people did not such things? Well, how did I know that they did not? It would be a secret that none would share openly with the world. Perhaps many people had already done what I was contemplating and had already experienced the delights of watching what their neighbours did in their moments of intimacy. I thought of my boyfriend and knew that he would never do such a thing. Yet, all too quickly, I put that thought from my mind. There were so many things after all that he would not do. Things that I wanted to do. Things that I needed. Things that I imagined a million other men would do and take pleasure from. I was not like him, I already had known that. Yet I realised then, that a great part of me did not want to even pretend to be like him any more, least of all to myself. I decided then, after hours of wondering, imagining, reasoning, that I would do exactly as I wanted, and if I were caught, the chances of which I thought were slim, I would simply blame the hole on my ineptitude in trying to fix a shelf that had come loose.

The decision to make the hole made, the only question that remained to be answered was – when? When I knew he was from home was the most straightforward answer. Yet how long would that mean waiting? Was he at home then? Even as I wondered, however, I heard the sound of voices in the hall and went to my peep hole and saw that at that very moment my neighbour coming back with not one but two beautiful young women, one on either arm. I could not wait, having seen that. I could not be responsible or respectable. I felt I simply must see then, that night, before my courage melted in the light of day and perhaps I gave up the scheme forever.

Very slowly, very carefully, trying not to make even the slightest sound, I took the hand drill from the box in the hall, padded back to my bedroom, pressed it to the wall above my bed and began to turn the handle. First plaster, and then some kind of crumbling brick whirled its way slowly back towards me along the drill-bit as I felt it working its way deeper and deeper into the wall. Though my fingers trembled as I did so, I pressed firmly but not so hard that when finally I was through the wall the drill-bit would come out jerking out the other side with a bang. Millimetre by millimetre I drove the drill deeper, then at last I felt the last resistance give way and I knew I was through. I froze where I stood on the bed and waited, my heart pounding, for some sign that my crime had been noticed. Yet none came. And so, summoning all of my courage, I wound the drill in tiny circles to widen the entrance on the other side and then drew it back, enlarging the tunnel I had made as I did so. When the drill was free, with so much excitement and fear that I wondered if my chest were about to explode with the pressure of trying to contain it, I leant forward and pressed my eye to the hole and saw the whole of my neighbour's living room spread out, before me. I could see the paintings on the far wall, and a large marble fireplace. I could see thick Persian rugs on the floor, and an immense leather sofa, and a dark wood bar, and long bay windows draped with curtains of deep blue velvet. Everything was softly lit by a fire in the hearth and by elegant antique lamps placed on side-tables of beautifully polished ebony, making it seem all the more luxurious and decadent. And then the three I had seen in the hall came into view, my rich neighbour in the middle, the two young women, one on either side, with his arms firm around their waists.

The two young women were both vividly attractive, almost to the point of unreality. They both seemed to move with a grace that I had never seen before in people; the grace of two stalking tigresses, or of two dressage ponies. Their dresses of black silk clung to their bodies in a way that filled me with a desperate, aching desire to touch them. And their figures beneath those dresses almost took the breath away. One of the young women was dark, her skin a tawny brown, with full lips and dark, smouldering eyes. Her legs were long and slender, her breasts large and full, of the sort that in my dreams I had imagined burying my face between, kissing, licking, feeling their silken smoothness pressing against my cheeks. The other was more petite, blonde, her hair worn in a high ponytail that accentuated her slender neck, her cheek bones and deep brown eyes beneath perfectly shaped brows and impossibly long lashes. Her figure was perfectly compact; her waist slim, her buttocks large and shapely and her small breasts standing firm and upthrust and clearly naked beneath the silk of her dress.

The man himself would have faded into nothingness beside them, I thought, were it not for the sheer power of his presence. He was not especially big, but he had an air about him that seem to magnify his size. He was the sort of man who, when he walked into a room filled with strangers, eyes would be drawn to him by the force of his personality along with looks of admiration and desire. He was dressed that night in a dinner jacket and open-collared shirt that seemed to fit his vaguely muscular frame like a glove. His grey flecked black hair was perfectly styled, and his tanned face with its bright green eyes, seemed curiously handsome and youthful in the warm orange light of the room. Watching them, I felt a tremor of excitement in my stomach and allowed my hand to drop to my breasts, to caress my already hardening nipples.

With a gentle push against the small of their backs, the man motioned the two young women toward the sofa, went himself to the dark-wood bar and took from it a bottle of champagne and three glasses. Going over to the sofa, he edged the women apart and sat down between them where with the touch of an expert he opened the bottle and poured them each a glass. Nothing had happened yet, but already I found myself almost more excited than I recalled ever having been with my boyfriend. I wanted something to happen in a way I rarely did with him, because what happened with him was so blandly predictable. I wanted them to forget the formalities, to forget everything and begin there and then to give me what I wanted to see. However, they did not immediately obey my will. Instead, they drank and spoke for a few minutes, and to increase my frustration, the words did not reach me through the hole in the wall. The young women were clearly flirting with him, I was sure of that. And he seemed to be charming them in return. Yet I noticed something through my frustration and eagerness that pleased me, even shocked me; there was not a hint of nervousness about any of them. No shame or reluctance or hesitance. They all seemed to be as comfortable in that situation, as they might have been drinking champagne with their oldest friend in the corner of a bar to which they had been regular visitors for many years passed.

I waited and watched until at last, just as I had begun to despair of seeing anything, the man seemed to have had enough of pleasant conversation and to want something more. He tossed off the remains of the champagne in his glass, and poured himself another, then sat back on the sofa and the women, seemingly in response to something he said, twisted in their seats to face him. From my place behind my peep hole I found myself smiling and I allowed my hand to fall from my breasts and slip into the silken thong I wore and to begin, very gently at first, to move over my sex.

Taking the blonde under the chin, the man raised her face to his and began kissing her, a long, lingering kiss. When finally he broke away, her cheeks were flushed. He turned to the other and kissed her too, and she returned the kiss hungrily, pressing her breasts against his chest and running her hands up his thighs. Then he brought them together and for a minute or two, they kissed one another passionately while he sat back and watched them, sipping his champagne. It was a perfect sight, beautiful and sensual and all the more thrilling for being real, not merely some pornographic film I had found and settled alone to watch. I felt myself grow wet beneath my fingers, and unconsciously my touching of myself became firmer.

When he seemed to have looked on long enough, the man leaned forward and said something and the young women separated once more. Both seemed faintly breathless, and each was smiling a smile imbued with passion. The man, meanwhile, leaned back once more and with large, strong-looking hands unbuttoned his trousers and drew out his cock, which itself was as large as any I had ever seen, and hard; achingly hard, its tip seeming to glisten in the soft light with the excitement of what he had already seen and with the anticipation of what was to come. Another phrase escaped his thick, sensual lips and then with one hand he had taken the dark woman by the back of her neck and gently guided her head down into his lap.

My breath caught in my throat and I watched with fascination as languidly, luxuriantly at first, the dark woman's tongue slipped out and began to run in long, slow strokes from the base of the man's cock to its very tip. Up and down she moved, causing the enormous weapon to grow harder and larger with every stroke. And then, when already he was squirming in his seat, thrusting it upward in a desperate attempt to receive more pleasure, she took the base in one hand and held it still as her lips and tongue engulfed the first six inches of it in one smooth motion. The man's head tilted back a moment, as though he were letting out a sigh of contentment, and then he returned to kissing the blonde woman with a new passion.

The dark woman kept up her ministrations, sucking him deeper and deeper into her mouth, then releasing him and flickering her tongue across his tip. And all the while he focussed his attention on the blonde, kissing her and running his hands over her body, then stripping off her dress and covering her breasts and pert nipples with yet more kisses. Oh, oh, I thought, watching him, feeling my own pleasure spread ecstatically through my body, if only I were her! How I wanted his lips on me, his tongue, his hot breath on my chest, his muscular body against mine.

Finally, perhaps fearing that he could hold out no longer under the dark woman's expert attentions, he raised her head and began to kiss her, passionately, gratefully, while the blonde, naked then beside him looked on. A minute passed, then, without breaking away from the dark woman, he took the blonde gently by the back of the neck just as he had her companion, and guided her down to take the place the dark woman had vacated. She seemed to do so even more eagerly than the dark woman had, plunging his straining cock straight into her mouth without stopping to kiss or lick or admire it. The man meanwhile, with confident movements, pulled down the shoulder straps of the dark woman's dress, and unveiled her breasts. And what breasts they were; large, and round and perfectly enhanced; the nipples dark and surrounded by great dark areola. As I would have sold my soul to do, he began urgently to kiss them, suck at them, tease them with his teeth, and in response I saw the dark woman fling her head back and let out her own sigh of ecstasy.

Unlike my own would have done, however, his worship of her breasts went on for a few minutes only. Then, with the blonde still sucking him deeply, he had the dark one stand up and dance for him. My god, but she knew how to dance, how to excite with only the tiniest movements of her body. Like an exotic tribeswoman, she entranced with only a seductive, rhythmical swaying of her hips, to which the black dress still clung, and a sensual caressing her bare breasts. I could have watched her dance forever I felt, but the man had different plans for her. At a word of command from him, her movements lessoned and she eased her dress over her thighs and allowed it to drop to the floor. The man smiled, his eyes running hungrily over her body. Then for a moment he raised the blonde's head for her to look at her companion too. She said something and smiled too, a lascivious, carnal smile. The man said something else and she replied to whatever it was with an even lustier expression lightening her face. And then he eased her head back into his lap and she went back to sucking him though her eyes kept flickering to the body of the dark woman. He gestured for the woman to turn and as she did so I saw to my mingled amazement and arousal, the woman's own very large, dark cock standing half-erect before me. I gasped and covered my mouth for fear of being heard, but remained transfixed by what I saw, drinking in the sight of the beautiful womanly body and the smooth, thick cock, feeling a new kind of desire trembling through me. What would it be like to be with a woman like that. A woman whose waist was narrow, hand's as delicate and fine as a young girl's, breasts large and sumptuous, arse turned to a fineness such as one only sees in paintings or airbrushed photographs, and the face of sultry angel, yet with a cock as thick and smooth firm as any man's; a cock which begged to be held, to be sucked, to be eased inside one where it would fill every inch with hot, throbbing pleasure. I trembled at the thought of touching it, of having it penetrate me and drive me to a climax, and between my legs my fingers quickened their dance, causing me to stifle moans of satisfaction and longing.

The man said something and the dark woman turned back to him abruptly, leaving me disappointed to be deprived of the sight that had so tantalised me. Then the man eased the blonde from him, raised her face to his and kissed her deeply and passionately while the dark woman swayed wantonly and caressed her breasts. At last he broke from the blonde and got up to stand beside the dark one. For a moment I thought he was going to reach down and take hold of her cock, to toy with it, feel it, stroke its smooth dark length just as I would have done, but to my disappointment he did not. He merely kissed her and took the full, dark-nippled breasts in his hands once more. The blonde meanwhile came over to where they stood, moving with the same dazzling grace as before and sank to her knees before them. Taking on cock in each hand, she began to stroke them slowly, examining them, pushing them together and rubbing them one against the other. Then she held them apart once more and took the woman's in her mouth. The woman seemed to tremble as those beautiful lips wrapped themselves around her.

      Oh, how I longed to be in the blonde woman's place! To be the one with the power to bring them pleasure or to withhold it as I wished; to tease them, drive them wild with the ecstasy I might at any time take from them. The dark woman seemed suddenly gripped with the fear that the blonde would indeed withdraw the pleasure she was lavishing upon her for I saw her wind her delicate, elegant, fingers through the blonde's hair and hold her where she was, beginning to control her movements, holding her one moment so that only the tip of her cock remained in the blonde's mouth, being bathed in the delights of the woman's willing tongue; the next moment easing the blonde down and down and down until her nose was pressing lightly against the curve of the dark woman's stomach. I wondered how she could fit it all in her mouth. I thought she might choke on it, or fight to break free, but to my amazement, far from fighting, I saw her tongue flicker out beneath the cock and begin to lick the dark woman's heavy balls where they hung against her chin even as every inch of it was buried in her mouth. I saw too that her eyes were glittering with lust and happiness. And all the while she performed her fellatio on the dark one, the blonde's other hand was jerking the man's cock with a steadily increasing rhythm while the man in turn kept up his worshipping of the dark woman's breasts. The picture of all these wanton pleasures combined was so perfectly decadent, so salacious and carnal that I could hardly believe it was real. It was like a dream; like one of my most sexually extravagant dreams, the sort from which I awoke sopping wet and almost mad with lust. Yet at the same time it was richer than anything I had ever dreamed, more amorous and erotic.

It was the man who broke the tableaux at last. Taking the blonde by the arm, he lifted her from her knees and between he and the dark woman they showered her lips and perfect little teardrop-shaped breasts with kisses. She was flushed and seemed breathless and happy and impassioned all at the same time. The man took her in his arms and carried her to the sofa and the dark woman followed and, picking up the bottle, poured a gentle stream of champagne over the blonde's body, which the man bent to lap up eagerly. Another stream followed the first and this time the dark woman joined the man, licking the cool, sparkling liquid from the blonde's breasts and stomach and thighs until the man had buried his head between her legs and begun caressing her sweet, shaven pussy with long, smooth, swirling strokes of his tongue. It was the blonde's turn then to grasp his head and hold him there, her hands gripping tightly, tightly, her eyes becoming liquid and then almost rolling back in her state of bliss. The dark woman meanwhile had wormed her way between the man's thighs and was sucking at his cock and balls while with one hand she squeezed those magnificent breasts together and with the other stroked her own cock, which had grown to be almost as large as the man's.

The scene went on thus, ecstatically, luxuriously, until the blonde began to claw at the smooth leather of the sofa and cry out with moans and screams of rapture that were audible even from where I stood behind my wall, my fingers buried in my sopping pussy, my eye watering from the intensity with which I stared through the peep hole, my body tremulous. Abruptly the man rose, breaking free of the blonde's grip on his head, and, placing himself on the sofa, he lifted the blonde on top of him, impaling her in one smooth, expert movement upon his great cock. She wailed with pleasure and began to ride him with a kind of frantic desperation. Yet, almost as soon as she had begun to do so, she was stilled by the dark woman, who had come behind her and placed her hands firmly on the blonde's shoulders. The blonde obediently desisted and leant forward against the chest of the man. The dark woman meanwhile leaned down and, for half a minute or more, bathed alternatively the lower shaft and balls of the man and the tiny, puckered anus of the blonde woman with luxuriant attentions of her tongue.

When both were shuddering beneath her, the dark woman reached over to her discarded handbag and took from it a tube of lubricant, which she slathered liberally over her own cock and the tight, rosebud of the woman's exposed anus. Then, with a delicacy and gentleness that a man would never have achieved, she began to ease her cock inch by inch into the blonde. The effect on the blonde woman was exquisite and palpable. At first she seemed to tense, biting her full and rosy lips between her teeth, but as soon as the dark woman was fully inside of her, stretching and filling her, she seemed to become imbued with a wild passion, and began riding and thrusting and slamming herself back on the two immense, beautifully hard cocks inside her in a kind of frenzy. Her cries and the cries of the dark woman and the deep moans of the man all rose together like the crescendo of a savage, carnal orchestra, and then the dark woman was pulling out and covering the blonde woman's back with arching tracks of sperm while the man simultaneously erupted within her sex and the blond shrieked and shook and clawed at the man's chest beneath her. For a moment, the dark woman merely slumped forward over the blonde, but then, as the man kissed the blonde woman with a gentle fervour, she slipped down to the blonde's sex from which the man's now softening penis had slipped, and licked up the come that flowed from it, with long, languid caresses of her tongue. The blonde shuddered and gripped the dark ones head against her for a long moment, and then pulled her up and kissed her passionately. Watching all of this, proved too much for me and brought rushing on my second orgasm, the first having stormed over me the moment the blonde had first mounted the man, and I sank onto my bed helplessly as it went thundering through every molecule of my body, raising me to previously unknown heights of bliss.

When my still quivering legs could support me again, I stood up and pressed my eye to the peep hole one last time and saw the three beyond dragging themselves from the sofa; the women to dress themselves with fingers that visibly trembled and chests that heaved; the man to go to the bar for more champagne, his legs, like mine, seeming barely able to hold him up. I watched them drink one last glass together, then kiss gently, gratefully, before the man showed the two women to the door.

Such conflicting emotions ran through me then. Guilt. Fear that what I had done might be discovered. And fear too of what I had felt watching the scene play out. Yet most of all overwhelming admiration for them; for having given themselves each to the other so passionately and so without restraint. And desire, I felt desire too; desire to be as they had been; to be so wild and exotic and commanding and willing to worship and be worshipped. Those last emotions dominated that fear and guilt almost completely. When I made love to my boyfriend the next day, I imagined that I was that blonde woman, that dark woman, that man, and the image brought me a pleasure that I had never before known. Yet, lying in bed afterwards, listening to the soft breathing of that boy who loved me beside me, I realised that I did not want only to *imagine,* as a normal person might be satisfied with doing. They had roused within me a wild desire to be like them, to be them, to find the pleasure that they had found – a dark forbidden pleasure – and to act with same beautiful voracity, the same unbounded passion as they had acted, showing neither shame nor fear nor uncertainty, only the most primal of desires.

# A FIRST EXPERIMENT WITH EXHIBITIONISM

After the night in which I had watched my neighbour, I became strangely obsessed with the desire to have others watch *me*. I went to the beach one day, alone, leaving my boyfriend to work in the city in the grey bank in which he had found a job. There on the beach, with the sun glittering on the water, and the sand warm even through my sandals, I walked along the shoreline until I found a slight hillock which could be seen for some distance on either side, and there I stopped and spread my towel. It was the hour for lunch and there were few people in sight, but, a little way from me, a group of young men and women lay together out on the sand. Most were looking down toward the water, there were two, however, a man and a woman, lying on their fronts, whose gaze, I thought, might well flicker now and then to my hillock. Placing my bag on the towel, I began, slowly, tantalisingly, I hoped, to undress. First I took off my shirt, unbuttoning it unhurriedly, button by button, allowing it to billow open in the light breeze, to reveal my body beneath. When it was fully undone, I let it drop and shook back my hair so that it no longer trailed across my breasts. Then I stripped off my shorts with what I imagined to be equally languid, sensuous movements, before stretching my arms high above my head as though to ease the tension of my body, though really to draw attention to my bare stomach and thighs. I turned my back on the group, doing so in a way that I hoped looked natural and not like the pirouette of a stripper, and when I was facing away from them, I bent double to undo the straps of my sandals and let them slide from my feet. Were they watching me, that man and woman? I wondered. Had they noticed me? Were they excited by what they saw; by the curve of my buttocks facing toward them, covered only by the thin strip of cloth of my bikini bottoms. Did the man feel a hardening of his penis? Did the woman look with disgust at my display, or with a faint tremor of arousal? Slowly I stood once more, and in one last gesture, a gesture of courage that I had previously not known myself to possess, I reached behind me and undid the strap of my bikini top and slipped it off, feeling the warm sea air play across my nipples as I did so. Then I turned to face the group, remaining upright for a moment only, giving anyone who wanted to look, a clear view of my naked breasts. Then finally I sank to my knees and stretched myself out on the towel.

The moment had been too brief for me to see whether the group had been watching. Yet I felt as though it had. I felt as though I could sense eyes running across my body and the feeling excited me. Between my legs I could feel a growing heat, accompanied by the faintest tremor of arousal. This was what life was supposed to be, I thought, full of strange, previously unknown thrills, and unfamiliar pleasures. It was supposed to be always new; new and a little dangerous. After a few minutes of lying there, however, to have simply given a glimpse of my body to those who might be watching did not seem enough. It had not satisfied me completely. I raised my head and looked at the group. The man and woman *were* looking at me, and talking animatedly; arguing it seemed to me. And another of the group, another man, had placed himself beside them and was looking at me too. I lay back and smiled. I had the audience I had been craving; a group who, though they might not admit it, could not help but look at me, just as I had been unable to resist looking at the gentleman in the flat next to mine. The feeling was spectacularly decadent and risqué. I do not recall anything quite like it. Even the gaze of a man about to make love to me, running over my naked body had never made me feel so wonderfully sexual or alive. I reached for my bag, and took from it a bottle of suntan lotion, then, raising the bottle above me, I squeezed a gentle trickle out over my thighs and stomach, before dripping a few final drops on first one breast and then the other. Then I placed the bottle down and began slowly to rub the cream into my skin, lovingly, caressingly, massaging it into my thighs and stomach first, and then raising myself a little on one elbow whilst keeping my face turned from the group and kneading the rest of the cream into my breasts. The sensation was wonderful. The touch of my hands on my naked skin. The cool, sweet smelling cream. The light breeze. And most of all the feeling of the eyes of those strangers on me, drinking me in. My nipples hardened and became sensitive, and between my legs, I felt that sweet ache, that throb of pleasure. Did I dare do more? I asked myself. Or should I simply leave it at that? But why should I? Why not draw from this moment, every ounce of pleasure it had to give. Lying back I eased my bikini bottoms over my hips and down my legs and finally kicked them off completely. Then I took more cream and dripped it, one drop at a time, onto my Mount Venus and the lips of my swollen sex. It felt heavenly; cold and light, but refreshing in the heat, and most of all sensual; exciting. Spreading my legs slightly, hoping that from where they lay my watchers would be able to make out the shaven lips of my pussy, opening slightly in arousal, I began to rub the cream into my sex. At first, I rubbed it only into my mound and into the soft skin around my lips but then I began to rub it into the lips themselves, squeezing them gently together, massaging them, opening them. A feeling of ecstasy flooded through me in waves. My finger brushed my clitoris, which throbbed beneath my touch. Then I began to play with myself, forgetting even to pretend that I was applying sunscreen. Gently, very slowly at first, I rubbed my hand in circles over my whole sex. Then, as my pleasure rose, I began to focus only on my clit. Faster and faster my fingers ran, their touch light and sensitive, yet dominating my whole body with the waves of bliss they created. With my other hand I began to pinch my nipples, to squeeze my breasts. I heard soft moans escape my lips, and then my fingers were moving frantically, driving pulses of ecstasy through every inch of my body. Finally, so suddenly almost that it took me by surprise, I was coming in a long, trembling, storming orgasm that seemed to go on and on and on. I cried out and clamped my hand over my sex as if to control it, to hold back the last cascading waves of pleasure. Yet I could not hold them back and instead felt them rush through me and over me and inside of me and I fell back onto the towel with my eyes closed, trembling and shaking, and every thought gone from my mind.

When I awoke, the sun was low in the sky and the group was gone. My skin felt tingly to the touch where a faint sunburn had spread over it. Yet I felt, at the same time, wonderfully free and alive and happy. Had the group still been there, I think I would have pleasured myself again, but they were gone and so instead I stood up and dressed and carried my bag back to the station to get the bus back into the city, thinking all the time of how it must have been for them to watch me, of what they must have thought and felt and desired, arousing myself anew with the simple imagining of their arousal. When I got home, I mentioned nothing of the incident to my boyfriend, but when I made love to him that night I felt myself doing so with a newly woken passion.

# A SECOND EXPERIMENT WITH EXHIBITIONISM

When I looked back the next day on my adventure at the beach, I found that in the cold light of morning the incident, though arousing still to the deepest degree, did not seem to me to be anything so very extraordinary. For those watching, what had they truly seen? A woman on the beach take off her clothes and rub suntan lotion into her body. That was the most natural thing in the world; not decadent at all or lascivious. I had pleasured myself in front of them, it was true. But looking back, I could not be sure that they had seen. They had been at some little distance from me. Perhaps they had seen the movements of my arms only, or even my hands moving over my body, but had they recognised these movements for what they were? Did they know that I had been pleasuring myself, bringing myself to that wonderful, explosive orgasm? Aware that I had done so intentionally where anyone might see? I could not even remember whether or not I cried out in my moment of ecstasy. Perhaps I did, or perhaps unconsciously I had stifled my cries. Even had I not, was it not possible that any moans or cries of pleasure had been blown away from them on sea breeze? That they had heard nothing? Oh, how frustrating it was not to know; not to know if I had truly lived out my fantasy of being watched, or no. I lay in bed after my boyfriend had left for work, playing the incident out in my mind over and over again, wishing that there was some way of confirming that the group had seen and understood and been shocked or aroused or had had any reaction at all to what I had done. Yet there was not. I would never see them again to ask. And had I seen them, I would never have had the courage to speak to them. Reluctantly, I made up my mind then that I could not truly consider the fantasy fulfilled; that if I wished it to be so, I must find some other way of exposing myself to the gazes of others in which there could be no question of them not seeing or not understanding. Even as I came to this conclusion, I found myself smiling and a familiar thrill ran through me. There was no disappointment to be found in the uncertainty, I felt, unless I left it at that one incident. If I were to repeat it, in another form, I could retain that first memory, and take pleasure from it in spite of its uncertainty, whilst augmenting it with one about what there could be no doubt. To allow no possibility of doubt, I would expose myself, I decided, here in the city, in the streets, where there could be no question of my behaviour being seen by anyone observing it as natural thing. And what was more, I made up my mind not to be timid as I realised I had been. At the beach, I realised, I should have placed myself closer to the group; close enough that they could see ever inch of my body, every movement of my fingers, every expression of pleasure that flowed across my face. Then I would have been certain. Now, I would not be so shy. I would make sure that I was close to those who would see me. Not at the end of a street, nor across a park, but almost beside them, close enough that if they had dared to do so they might almost reach out and touch me, caress me. I wanted to pleasure myself merely thinking about what might take place. However, I did not. I resolved to wait and thereby gain an excitement, a thrill, more exciting and tangible than that which I would receive were I to have satisfied my desires there and then, alone in my bed.

      I showered hurriedly, eager to go before my courage failed me, but I dressed with peculiar care. In my drawers I found a beautiful, delicate pair of black, crotchless silk panties that I had never dared to wear, and a matching bra whose cups were entirely transparent, and put them on. I thought to begin with of accompanying the underwear with a skirt, which I might allow to ride up while sitting, and a shirt whose buttons I could leave open down to the waist and then finally a long black coat on top. But as I looked for them in the wardrobe I realised that to do so would be cowardly and so instead I put on thigh length black stockings, high heels and the long black coat and nothing else. In front of the mirror, I examined myself, nervously to begin with, but then with satisfaction. I do not say that I am beautiful, but in that moment I felt myself to be eminently desirable. I felt like a cabaret dancer, or a high class prostitute, or like a woman modelling in the photos in the windows of an expensive lingerie boutique. My skin was gently tanned from the beach and seemed to glow, to beg to be touched and kissed. My breasts, not bare yet still unveiled, looked at once inviting and untouchable. Meanwhile the heels and stockings made my legs appear much longer, slimmer and more elegant. And the last touch, the panties themselves, framed my sex perfectly, causing its lips to seem more luscious and pouting; more inviting to tongues and fingers. Yes, I thought, this is what I wanted, this is what I had truly imagined; to be desirable, to be beautiful and seductive, and at the same time to be completely powerful, in control, able to give glimpses of myself to strangers that would haunt them for a long time afterwards, when I wanted, when I chose, and to conceal myself or cut those glimpses short equally as I chose.

In the street I felt myself walking with a confidence that I had never before felt myself to possess. I saw myself passing in shop windows and smiled at the elegant and seductive woman who looked back at me. In the crowds, I felt marvellously alive. There I was, surrounded by people who were completely unaware that beneath the folds of my coat there was nothing but silken lingerie that hid nothing, restrained nothing, locked away nothing. I thrilled as a man brushed against me on the pavement and then turned to apologise. I could have opened my coat then and allowed him to see me, to feast his eyes on my body, but I did not need to in order to feel the power I held. Two young women stopped me to ask me directions, and again the same thrill ran through me. What would they feel, if they knew? Would they be shocked? Or aroused? Or jealous? Or inspired to do the same? I imagined for a moment them doing same, and the idea caused me to feel my cheeks flush faintly as a tremor of desire ran through me. Oh, that everyone were as I was in that moment, I thought. How exciting the world would be then.

Having walked through the streets for a time, I went to café in the Plaza del Campillo and sat on the terrace and ordered coffee. In front of me there three other occupied tables. At one sat a man in his forties dressed in a very smart business suit, with a handsome, distinguished face and a mop of dark hair. At another, there was a couple in their twenties, the girl dressed in a floaty summer dress that revealed nothing of her but a vague hint at her figure, while the boy wore a tight black tee-shirt, the arms turned up over muscular biceps and the air of the sullen rebel. At the last table, an older couple sat across from one another, each reading the newspaper. Both the businessman and the rebel glanced across at me and then away; the businessman subtly, inoffensively; the rebel boldly, the expression in his fine dark eyes one of confidence that, had he wanted to, he might have any woman in the world. I liked that look, as I did the look of polite interest of the other. Most of all, however, I liked the idea of how each might change when I did what I had planned to do.

The waiter brought my coffee and a glass of water and I thanked him and smiled at him before he went back inside. When I was alone once more, I sank back more comfortably in the wicker chair, and stretched my legs out in front of me allowing the tails of my coat to rise up my thighs – not too much, but just enough to cause anyone looking to wonder if I were wearing anything beneath it. I saw the businessman's eyes flicker back in my direction and freeze for a moment on my legs before he looked away. The rebel was looking at the girl with whom he was with. I wanted him to look at me. As I drank my coffee I allowed myself to slip further down, very gradually and naturally in my chair pulling the stiff fabric of my coat higher and higher with the movement until the tops of my stockings were showing. I noticed that some of the passers-by were looking at me as they went by, their expressions a mixture of hunger and disapproval. The businessman, meanwhile, did not seem to be able to stop glancing across at me. Every time he did so, he blushed a little and looked quickly away. Yet a moment or so later he would always glance again. His discomfort and arousal and temptation, and the fact that I was the cause of them all, that I was tantalising him, teasing him, excited me. I could feel myself growing hot between my legs, and my nipples were hardening against the fine, lacy fabric of my bra. But I wanted the rebel to look most of all. And then he did. He looked briefly, his eyes flickering toward me and then away, but in that moment he had obviously caught a glimpse of my bare thighs above my stockings, because he looked back almost immediately with a slight raise of his eyebrows and a curious brightness in his eyes. I smiled inwardly and began to feel slightly breathless. I drank the rest of my coffee and called the waiter for the bill. When I had paid it, I picked up the glass of water and drained it very slowly, and as I did, I opened my legs inch by inch, causing the tails of the coat to slip from my thighs revealing their bare tops, and my black lace of my panties, and my hot, pouting sex. The businessman blushed deep red and shifted in his seat as though trying to conceal a sudden erection. The rebel meanwhile kept looking boldly at me, his eyes running over my thighs and pussy with an intensity so palpable that I felt for a moment as though I could feel him caressing me, touching me, toying with me. His gaze flickered to my face, and his eyes met mine, wide and full of desire. I winked at him with a fearlessness that I had not known myself to posses and saw him almost blush too before his eyes dropped, irresistibly to my sex once more. For a moment I let them both look, then I reached down and with one finger touched myself with a long stroke, feeling my wetness as I did so. And then I rose, closed my coat once more and walked away, down the long avenue of the Carrera de la Virgen almost trembling with excitement as I went.

For the rest of that morning, I sought others to tempt and toy with. In a bar, I gave a glimpse of my breasts to a waiter, who almost dropped his tray in surprise. By the fountain, I paused and bent over to straighten the straps of my shoes, allowing my coat to fall completely open as I did so, while a group of tourists looked on in excited amazement. The man at the tobacco kiosk saw my near-naked body as I looked in my pocket for change, as did the pretty young saleswoman in the perfume shop. In the eyes of everyone to whom I exposed myself, I felt that I saw the same mixture of shock and incomprehension, and arousal, and in seeing it each time the dark thrill, the sense of my own power, the throb of my arousal, seemed to intensify.

In the afternoon, it grew hot and I went to the Paseo del Salon where I sat myself on a bench by the fountain in the shade of an orange tree. I was growing tired, and by then almost mad with a desire to bring my state of arousal to a peak, to pleasure myself or be pleasured, and enjoy the miraculous bliss of the orgasm I had felt building within me all day. One more, I told myself, and I would go home. One more, to remember, and then my fantasy would be fulfilled.

As if on cue a couple came and sat down on the bench across from me. We were separated by the fountain, yet the fact that there was no-one else in sight and that the trees and low hedges and flowerbeds seemed to cut us off from the rest of the world, created an intimacy, a closeness, appearing to cut the distance to almost nothing. The couple were young and attractive. The woman had beautiful dark hair, cut in a bob above her shoulders, deep black eyes, rosy lips, and a slim body that looked very tanned against the white tee-shirt she wore and the pale blue cut-off jeans. The young man meanwhile, had a slightly rounded face, glittering eyes, a dark stubble beard and a muscular looking body concealed beneath an open necked shirt. He smiled at me through the spray of the fountain and replied to the young woman, who was sitting sideways on on the bench, facing him, without turning away. Feeling the tightness of fear in my chest, and the tremble of excitement rising through my sex and stomach to my breasts, I slowly undid the belt of the coat, and even more slowly, barely an inch at a time, I drew it open, never breaking my eye-contact with the young man, until my whole body, my breasts in the see-through bra, my legs, my stomach, my pussy, were all exposed to view. His eyes ran over me and widened and I saw his smile freeze, then broaden. He turned and said something to the young woman and, before I could close the coat, she was looking at me too. For a moment, I thought I would see in her face outrage or jealousy, but I did not. Instead, she smiled too, languidly, erotically, and her eyes seemed to glitter.

With a mixture of excitement and horror, I watched her twist away from the young man, get to her feet and come directly across to me until she stood over me. I looked up at her almost fearfully, afraid of what she might do. Would she hit me? Or scream at me? Or abuse me? Would she threaten to call the police? She did none of these things, however. She merely looked down at my body, running her eyes over every inch of it, and sank to her knees in front of me.

"Do you mind?" she asked, her voice deeper than I had expected, and at once kind and sultry. And then, before I had replied, she had leant forward and I felt her lips on my chest, kissing slowly, gently down over my breasts and stomach until finally they grazed the silk of my panties. Then she was kissing me between my thighs, her tongue running slowly at first and then with more urgency, more strength more speed, all over my sex. I felt her tongue penetrate me. And then her mouth was sucking at my clit while her tongue moved to lap at it, to circle it, to massage it, driving a sudden, uncontrollable blossoming of pleasure racing up from my sex through every part of my body. Unconsciously, I found that I had taken hold of her head, entwining my fingers in the silken waves of her hair, pressing her hot, eager mouth harder and harder against me. I moaned, and then cried out, and my head went back. I caught a glimpse of the young man, still on his bench but now with his hard, thick cock in his hand, masturbating it, while he stared at the spectacle in front of him. And then I was coming, in a long, earth-trembling orgasm that went on and on, sweeping with it all of the pleasure, the anticipation, the arousal of the day into one, perfect, unbelievably powerful climax. At last, I found myself slumped back on the bench and the woman had raised her head and was gently closing my coat with small, delicate fingers. Then she rose to her feet and leaned over to kiss me. I kissed her back as though in a dream, tasting myself on her lips, sweet and fragrant, loving the gentleness of her kisses and the soft, pillowy feel of her lips. And then she was gone, crossing back to her lover and, taking him by the hand, and leading him away through the trees and out of sight. For myself, I could no more have got to my feet than I could have climbed Mount Everest in that moment. I simply lay back, feeling the warm current of my pleasure rippling over me and dissipating into the hot afternoon air. "That was real," I thought vaguely as I lay there, "and no-one, not even myself, can take it from me."

# THE SURPRISES AND PLEASURES OF A COUNTRY NIGHT

From the stories that proceed this, it might be assumed that I had been a late developer in love; that I had previously always repressed my more hedonistic desires. Yet that was not entirely the case. A number of times I had given into them; had let my passions lead my actions rather than giving my fears the lead; had acted in the way that I desired to act, not the way that I thought I should act to be seen in the eyes of others as we are supposed to want to be seen. My first time with a man was an example of that.

He was a young man, a few years older than me, who I was introduced to at a party. He was blond and handsome and when he spoke his eyes seem to penetrate my being, just as his laugh sparked joy in me and his touch excitement. I think I had known no more than two hours, before I knew that I wanted him to be my first, and sought to make it so.

His car was parked a way along the private road that led down to the house where the party was taking place, almost at the ridge of the hill that over-looked it. To get there, we had to walk almost blindly through the avenue of old trees, through whose spreading foliage barely a ray of moonlight trickled. I remember that all the way he was speaking, yet seemingly with no clue as to what he was saying. He was looking at me as he spoke, and I looked back at him with his pale, beautiful face and his very blond hair seeming to glimmer in the half-light, and with the slim waist, and broad shoulders and the large, chiselled arms, swinging tantalisingly close to me, and my thoughts had no connection with the words that were coming out of his mouth. Instead they were all of how I wanted to touch him, to feel his body pressed against mine; to have him kiss me and undress me and take me. He walked so close beside me, now and then brushing against me with his hand or hip, the subtle aftershave he wore, wafting faintly, seductively to me on the still night air. Sometimes I replied to whatever nonsense he was jabbering, but I had the impression that he hardly caught my words; that my voice, along with noise of the party and faint swish of the wind moving through the trees, drifted from him into the darkness, without leaving any lasting impression.

When finally we had reached the car, I moved closer to him and half-murmured, half-whispered the thought that was in my mind, and was, too I felt, sure to bring some reaction out in him. "I feel so slutty," I said, "that I have left a party with you, hoping that you are going to fuck me in your car." And those words did indeed seem to break through whatever tumult of words and thoughts and images that had been running through his mind. Perhaps until that moment, he been suffering under the delusion that I had not thought for a moment of that in agreeing to go to the car with him, as he had suggested, to find some cigarettes for me. I was sure that he had had such an intention, of course, or at least such a hope. Yet I imagine that until that moment he had felt that it were the sort of hope that would require a great deal of work, of seduction, of words and gentle caresses, to bring to fruition. Yet to hear that no seduction was necessary, to hear me say so frankly and with a husky note of desire in my voice, caused his eyes to begin to glitter with a strange fire.

Once at the car, he opened the door for me and pulled the seat forward and I slipped passed him into the back. In turn, he opened the driver's door, leaned into the front and, switching on the ignition, turned on some soft music, before following me, eagerly. There was not much space, but with the other seat forward, there was enough. No sooner was he beside me than I reached over and kissed him; a small kiss first. Then I kissed him again and again, and his lips opened under mine and I felt the tip of hot, gently tongue flicker against mine. With one hand he cradled my head, running his fingers through my hair, while with the other he reached out to unbutton my dress.

"You will take it slowly, won't you?" I whispered, between kisses, excited, but at the same time nervous, fearful. It was after all my first time. I was not afraid of the pain of penetration, as many girls are, since I had pleasured myself not just with my fingers, but with toys that I had bought illicitly and smuggled into my bedroom, small ones at first, then larger as I had grown braver, and the vestiges of pain were no more than a dim memory to me. Yet I was nervous still, of putting myself into the hands of another, or being naked before someone who might look at me and see beauty, or something else, who might be inspired to pleasure by me, or disappointed by me. I wanted him to please me, yet I wanted to please him too, as much or more than anyone else he had been with had done. I wanted him to remember me, as I wanted to create memories of my own that were worth retaining.

"We can go as slowly as you like," he replied, his voice and deep and indescribably sexy in that moment. I wonder looking back, whether he were not thinking to himself then that my hesitance was feigned; that it was merely a part of the seductive charm I sought to employ in such situations. Or perhaps, that it was merely what I believed men wanted to hear; that they wanted most of all to believe that those they were taking were giving themselves only to them, not to the many who wanted them. I do not believe that he thought me truly innocent. In fact I know he did not.

  The buttons of my dress came undone one by one, exposing the white bra beneath. There was more light there, above the avenue, and looking down, I could see faintly the curves of my breasts, appearing to strain against the thin fabric which barely seemed sufficient to contain them. To me they looked desirable. Yet, in that moment, it was more important to me that they seemed desirable to him. To be made love to by someone who did not think me beautiful, was not part of any fantasy I had ever had.

Breaking free from my lips, he bent low to kiss gently across my shoulders and down into my cleavage where the flesh was soft and welcoming, then across the cups of my bra, kneading the breast he was not kissing, gently. The sensation sent a tingling of excitement through me; of excitement and pleasure, and a tiny sigh escaped my lips, followed by another. He kissed back to my shoulders and slid the straps of my bra and dress down my arms, kissing the silken skin beneath as he did so. Then, he returned to my breasts and, pulling the fabric down, unveiled them one by one, kissing around and across my nipples and finally sucking each in turn into his mouth where his tongue ran in tight, swirling circles around them, seeming to send rippling pulses of erotic joy through my body and driving any fears I had had from me. My nipples rose quickly to his ministrations, hardening and lengthening until their tips stood out almost an inch from the light pink areolae around them; and every part of them became hypersensitive, magnifying his caress a hundred times over. I reached behind myself, and the bra came off, followed by the top half of the dress, and I was in his arms again, kissing him fervently while his hands massaged my breasts and his fingers lightly pinched my nipples, driving me wild with a desire for more.

I noticed that my breathing had started to come in shallow, rapid bursts, while my hand, seemingly of its own accord, had taken hold of the back of his neck as though to prevent him escaping or ceasing those delightful kisses he showered upon me. Every time he gently pinched a nipple, twisting it lightly, a moan escaped from me, as a burst of new pleasure spread from my breasts down through my stomach and into that place between my legs, that was already growing hot and eager for caresses. When finally he reached down toward the white panties which had been revealed by my falling dress, my legs opened to receive him. My pussy was dripping wet, the coarse hairs slicked down against the skin. At the touch of his fingers I moaned louder, and thrust my hips forward, grinding myself in a circle against his hand, relishing this new sensation, that of being given pleasure rather than lavishing it upon oneself. In the face of my eagerness, he seemed to become more animated and he pushed me back against the seat and manoeuvred himself with difficulty in the cramped space until he was on his knees between my legs with his face pressed against my pussy. The scent of sex filtered up to me, faint yet fragrant. I was sure that the heat emanating from me must have been noticeable to him even before his mouth touched me. And then he was kissing my upper thighs, and his tongue ran first over the soft skin around my pussy lips, then over my lips and then he was sucking me into his mouth while his tongue flickered across my engorged clitoris, causing a pulsation of amorous joy to run through me. I moaned and squirmed in my seat and taking him by the hair forced his head further down, and spurred on by this, he preceded to kiss and lick and suck every inch of me from my mons to the cleft between my buttocks, before returning to my clitoris with a passion. I was bucking against him by then, rocked by the first tremors of an orgasm, letting out wailing moans and driving my nails almost into his scalp as I fought to push him harder and harder against me until he must almost have been suffocating in the dripping, sweet-tasting folds of my sex. And then I was coming, a great orgasm, more powerful than any I had brought myself, thundering through me in a trembling, almost unbearable storm, that left me jerking and writhing on the seat, yet did not seem to end, but only to throb on, less powerfully after a minute or so, yet still there, still vibrating deep within me.

As he lifted his head, I think perhaps he expected me to be slumped back and temporarily out of action, but I was not. I wanted no pause, but only more pleasure. I snatched his head toward me, kissing my own juices from his face and lips. Then, with a sudden strength that I did not know myself to possess I forced him back and with fumbling hands tore open his belt and flies and wrenched out his hard, throbbing cock. Though I had never done so before with any man, I bent over and buried as much of it as I could fit into my mouth, as I had seen pornstars do, and with squelching and choking sounds began sucking it in a frenzy. The sensation was wonderful, powerful, intoxicating, as were moans that came from him, the tension I felt spreading through the prominent muscles of his legs and stomach where my hands trailed over them. Yet, much as I wanted to please him, I wanted my own satisfaction far more. Thus, almost as quickly as I had begun, I stopped, rose, and swung my leg over him and impaled myself on that smooth, thick tool, beginning immediately to ride him as though my life depended on it. My head was flung back and my breasts upthrust into his face; my arms supporting me on the headrests behind. And it was as though all of my actions, my movements, were given over then into the power of bliss. From the very moment he entered me, I began to come again, and that feeling went on and on, building rather than dissipating, growing ever more explosive and voracious. At first he gripped my arse to aid my movements, but then quickly his hands and lips returned to my breasts, which were bouncing, shapely and firm in front of his face in such a way that seemed to make resistance to their temptations an impossibility. And all the while he caressed me, I rode him with greater and greater fervour, sliding up and down his length, rising so high that several times he slipped out, only to be thrust back in with a trembling hand, until finally my orgasm reached once more again in a trembling, shrieking peak which caused me to slow my movements only for a moment to catch my breath, and for my vision to return, and to sweep my hair back from my face, before beginning again. It seemed that I might have gone on like that for ever, but such violent passion brought him suddenly to edge of the abyss from which there is no turning back….

"I'm going to come," I heard him hiss almost despairingly through gritted teeth, and to my own surprise I reacted by slipping quickly off him onto the floor beside him, where I took his bulging, rock hard cock in my hand and began jerking it frenziedly, desperate to bring him the same wild ecstasy he had brought me. The first shot of come burst from him and slapped against my cheek, yet this only caused me to move my hand faster. A second jet squirted across my chin and lips and a third and fourth and fifth cascaded out, hitting my face and upthrust breasts indiscriminately, before finally the flow ebbed and my hand slowed to no more than a gentle toying. He leaned over then and kissed me, running his tongue over my lips before caressing my own with it, urging me to taste him. I kissed him back fervently, enjoying my first taste of the strange, sweet-salty liquid and, encouraged by this, he kissed my cheeks and chin and breasts, sucking up the sperm which coated them and transferring it drop by drop into my mouth. When I had drunk it all, I sighed deeply, then finally crawled back into my seat and lay there with my head back and my eyes closed.

"I never knew," I heard myself say, in a voice that seemed to come from somewhere far away, "that my first time would be like that. My first time with a man…"

"My God!" he blurted out, seeming to snap back from the dreamlike trance that had followed his orgasm, and looking at me in wide eyed astonishment. "If that was your first time, what will your second time be like?"

I did not reply, but merely kissed him, yet in my imagination a blissful collage of images of licentiousness, ardour, and rapture was playing out. It would be a long time before those images became corporeal, it turned out; but even then I wanted them to.

# THE CINEMATIC EVENING

My experiments with exhibitionism did not have the effect that I had expected. I had thought that by giving myself so fully to a single fantasy, by indulging in it without restraint or hesitation, I would be cured of all fantasies, able to put them from my mind and to go back to living a normal life, or to the image at least of how I imagined a normal life should be. The effect, however, was quite the opposite. Having freed myself from the fear of committing an act I had previously seen as taboo, I had not banished fantasy in general from my mind, but rather had fuelled it. Other, darker fantasies began to haunt me, more daring fantasies, more exciting and lascivious. When I made love to my boyfriend, I found that hardly thought of him at all any more. The moment he touched me, or kissed me, or entered me, my mind was transported into the midst of a whirling mass of stories and pictures, full of strangers and excitement. His caresses gave me pleasure, yet I no longer felt them to be his caresses. To me, they were the caresses of a boxer whom I nursed and gave myself to after a big fight; of a handsome, unknown man who took me roughly, almost against my will, in train carriage into which anyone might enter at any moment; of a man who was paying me for my body; of an older woman – a teacher or therapist – who betrayed the ethics of her trade by seducing me. It was not the shy, kind, retiring boy who worked in the bank and worried about my happiness who took me. It was his boss taking me on his desk in a fit of passion, or the driver of a taxi, or an aristocrat who kept me as his pet and led me around with a diamond encrusted collar about my neck. Night after night, I made love to the painter for whom I modelled, or the man who employed me to look after his children, to policemen and pilots, belly-dancers and street walkers, soldiers going away to war and Arab Sheiks who had captured me, but never to my boyfriend who loved me so slavishly.

Then one night I was walking through the city, dressed in nothing but a long coat and high-heels, when a sudden wild desire to give myself to a stranger took hold of me. Not to fantasise about doing so, as I had done so often with my boyfriend. But to really do so. I wanted to find someone who did not know me, who did not even know my name, and not to talk to him but to wordlessly seduce him, to intoxicate him with my sensuality, and then to pleasure him and run from him with no explanation, or promise of seeing him again, thereby leaving him to wonder forever who the woman who had given him such bliss so mysteriously had been. The idea thrilled me with that dark thrill of forbidden pleasure. I could feel my body almost trembling with desire and anticipation, and my cheeks flush with colour. But where could I find such a man? In a bar? But then he would want to talk to me. In the street? There the same would be true. I thought for a moment of going into a men's bathroom and taking the first man I found alone, but then I changed my mind. The image of that was too cheap, too dirty; it lacked the romance of mystery I wanted. I found myself walking back and forth in front of the fountain in Plaza del Campillo almost mad with unsated desire. Suddenly the answer came to me and I could have cried out with relief and joy. Retracing my steps I went to the Art-House cinema on the Carretera de la Virgen and, with hands that shook with excitement, bought a ticket to a film that had just begun. The cinema was almost always three quarters empty. They showed foreign films and surrealist films and sensual, melodramatic love stories with plots that ended in disappointment and tragedy, and the public at large stayed away. I had been there before, however, and I remembered that I had seen several brooding looking intellectuals sitting alone in the shadows, watching whatever film was showing with obvious fascination. That was the sort of man I wanted. A quietly passionate man, who understood romance and sensuality, but who had a trace shyness running through him; the sort of man who would never have dreamt of such a thing happening to him, and who afterwards would try to rationalise it, to understand it, to find some profound meaning in it, yet in doing so would always relive the action and therefore never be able to escape it or avoid being marked by it.

In the theatre itself, the lights were dim, the film on the screen showing a love scene in black and white, dark and sensual. I paused in the entrance and looked slowly around. There were my intellectuals, spaced out in the lines of plush velvet seats. There were several couples also, sitting together in the shadows; some kissing, some holding hands, others merely staring ahead. From these, I looked away, scanning instead the figures of the lone strangers. Which should it be? Which would be most grateful? Which was most attractive? My stomach tightened as I tried to make my choice. A part of me could not believe what I was considering. Was I really going to choose a stranger, place myself beside him and without speaking or seeking to know him, initiate the most intimate of encounters? Could I? Was I brave enough? I was before I came inside, I told myself. Now, I must be again, or else I would regret it later, hate myself for not having the courage to give myself over to one of the pleasures I craved.

Marshalling my courage, I scanned the room again. Several of the men did not attract me all. They were good-looking enough for the most part, but they seemed arrogant – the type that might even be expectant of such an encounter occurring; who would congratulate themselves for it and boast to their friends about it, yet never haunt themselves with trying to understand it. Several others I dismissed too because they did not seem clean, or desirable. Then finally my eyes lit upon a man in the very centre of the room, alone and with several empty rows between him and anyone else. From what I could make out of him in the shadows, he looked handsome, but in a very shy and boyish way. He wore an elegant suit jacket with a tee-shirt beneath, and had wavy brown hair of the sort that mothers always desire their sons to have and keep. His profile, which was all I could make out of his face, was handsome too, finely shaped, clean shaven and adorned with the expensive, stylish glasses of the bohemian. He was perfect. Even the eager flickering movements of his hands on the arms of the chair in which he sat were attractive and shy and sensual all at once.

Hesitating no longer, I walked quickly down the aisle, afraid that if I did not I would lose my nerve and turn back, and then edged my way along his line of seats and took the one next to him. He glanced up at me as I sat down, and a smile of surprise flickered momently across his face. Then the surprise changed to something like shy happiness, and he nodded politely to me before turning back to the screen. I felt an almost overwhelming desire to immediately reach over and touch him, but I resisted. I did not want him to take fright or to speak. So instead of touching him, I settled myself in the chair, allowing my coat to open across my thighs and turned my attention to the film. I felt nervous still, uncertain, but the power of my excitement was greater and I no longer wanted to run away. I merely waited as the film played on. It was a love story about a couple whose love for some reason I could not understand was prohibited. Her family opposed it and wanted her to marry someone else. His own family seemed to want to send him abroad, to make a new life for himself. Yet they would not allow themselves to be parted. At night they would slip from their respective windows and cross the meadow that lay between their houses, and kiss and embrace and then run together, hand in hand, through the meadow and into the shadows of the forest beyond. There they would wander beneath the trees, talking and planning their escape. Kissing sometimes, taking one another in their arms, but shying away for a long time from doing anything further. It felt wonderfully appropriate alongside the story that was playing out in my mind. I wanted to touch the man beside me, to reveal my naked body to him beneath my coat. I wanted to have him touch me, lightly, teasingly. Yet still I did not dare. I merely stayed where I was, feeling his body close beside me, catching the faintest scent of an expensive aftershave coming from him; sensing, rather than seeing, as he moved in his seat, but doing no more.

When the couple finally came together, they did so in the bedroom of a rundown hotel. They came in from the rain and began to slowly to undress one another and to dry each other on soft white towels, carefully, romantically, uncertainly. I felt the man beside me shift again in his seat, and I allowed my legs to open a little further so that my thigh grazed against his. He moved away, perhaps having hardly noticed it, but when he shifted again, I once more allowed my thigh to graze his and this time, he glanced at me as if to apologise. My moment had arrived, I remember realising. I put my finger to my lips to hush him and smiled at him. Then I reached down and opened my coat completely so that my naked body lay out in front of him, gleaming palely in the light from the screen. His eyes became very large. He moved back an inch, yet his gaze continued to run over me, eagerly, uncomprehendingly, almost desperately. I smiled again, and this time I took his hand in mine, lifted it gently and cupped it to one of my breasts. I heard him gasp, but I did not let him go. His hand was warm and dry, larger than I imagined, large enough to hide my whole breast from view. I moved his fingers encouragingly, and almost painfully nervously he began to caress my breast, feeling its weight, tracing its form with his fingertips before finally massaging it beautifully and tenderly. I felt a thrill run through me as he touched me. It was all I had wanted. With my own hand, I reached over and very slowly undid his flies and took out the cock that had lain hidden within. It was long but slim, already hard to the touch. He gasped again as I touched it, tracing my fingers up and down its length. Then I released him and taking his hand I moved it slowly down my body until it was resting on my sex.

His lithe, elegant fingers were uncertain, unpractised. It did not matter, however. So aroused was I by the situation, by the dim lights and shadows, by the soft velvet chairs and indistinct figures in the other rows, by the feeling of by committing some risky, dangerous, taboo act; by the fact that he was a stranger, whose face I had not even seen clearly, that my pleasure grew and grew, coursed through my body bringing it to life, sensuous and tingling almost instantly. His pace remained gentle, hesitant, for what felt like a long time as he explored every millimetre of me, seeming to delight in my wetness, in the heat pulsing from me. Then, in the very moment in which I had begun to pray that he would find my clitoris and stay there, he did so, and as if in surprise at its engorged form, his pace quickened suddenly and dramatically. I reached for his hand to still it, wanting to draw out the moment, to languish in it, but already it was too late. Without warning, my orgasm swept through me, causing every inch of my body to shake and cry out with ecstatic joy, forcing me to bite hard on my lips to keep from making a sound. And then it was passed, leaving behind it only a deep, throbbing tremor. I pushed his hand away then and kissed him. I wanted to bring him joy, to drive him wild as he had driven me, to tease him and torment him with bliss, before finally letting him experience the perfect pleasure that I had just experienced. Yet, like myself the situation seemed to have proved too much for him to bear. I bent over and took his long, hard cock in my mouth, and almost the moment my lips made contact with him, he tensed and let out a repressed groan and I felt his come shoot out over my tongue and flood my mouth in a series of long, hot jets. I went on sucking him until he grew soft, swallowed his milky seed and then released him and kissed him once more on the lips, before getting up and hurrying up the aisle, out of the theatre and out of the cinema and into the street. Outside, I adjusted my coat and checked my face in my compact to make sure that no droplet of semen had escaped my lips and remained to betray what I had just done. The face that looked back at me was flushed and happy. And, beyond its happiness, there was something else too – a power, a new found air of confidence; a force of life. It was the face of someone who recognised their desires, I thought, and was not afraid to give in to them, and I was proud that that face was mine.

# THE INTERVIEW

When I left school, and left my home town behind, I lost touch, intentionally or through lazy ambivalence, with all but one of my friends from those day. That friend, Carina, I kept in touch with only because she liked to call me at least once a week to tell me gossip about all of the people I had once known. Whether I wanted to hear this, was not something that she had ever asked me. Mostly, the gossip was nonsense and the very fact of listening to it bored me. There were times, however, when it was something well worth the hearing, and these times compensated for the usual tedium and kept me from ignoring her calls, or changing my number.

One story she told me, I remember in particular, partly because of its content, which as you will see was memorable in the extreme; partly because I have often wondered looking back, whether it had an influence on some of the choices that I have made myself, unconsciously of course. That story regarded one of her friends, a pretty dark thing a few years below us, who had turned nineteen just a few months before, and had come to stay with Carina for a few days before going back to London where she had been living for several months. When her name was first mentioned, I searched my memory and found that, to my surprise, I remembered her quite clearly. An image of her jumped into my mind. She had dark eyes and thick lips and a figure that was somewhere between lithe and curvaceous; slightly short legs, a round, pert arse narrowing to a slim waist and, above, a pair of pointed breasts whose exact size was hard to discern due to the clothes she wore. She seemed pretentious and affected in all things and when I had still lived in the town I had never chosen to spend time with Carina when she and Carina were together. The friend had always carried herself as though she were somehow superior to all those around her; purer, more worthy of admiration. She treated those she had known, with a haughtiness that suggested that she was aware they desired her, whether they did or not, and that they had no hope of having her. Everything about her, every look and movement, projected the idea that someone like her could never be touched by lesser beings. That it was a facade, I did not doubt. Yet it annoyed me nonetheless and I remember how fervently I had hoped that it would not rub off on Carina. The story that Carina told me, however, assured me that it was desperately unlikely that Carina would try to emulate her, whilst at the same time confirming my suspicions that the friend was not what she pretended to be. Strangely, however, it also made me rather desirous of seeing her again.

During the course of her visit her friend had confided to Carina that she had started escorting in London and had been doing it now for some months.

"She told me all about it," Carina told me, a mixture of shock and excitement in her voice. "She said that there are all sorts of things you have to do well, especially pleasing people with your mouth, and she said that she is not sure if she wants to continue because she does not really like doing that. She told me that the clients have you dress up as all sorts of things and play out all sorts of roles for them; pretend to be a school girl or another man's wife, or their sister, or a slave they bought on the internet. All sorts of strange and dirty things. She told me all about the interview she had to have before they would let her join the agency she works for too. It sounded awful."

I felt a thrill tremble through me at that moment as a series of imagines suddenly began to rush into my mind; images of wanton depravity, of humiliations, of unrestrained lust, of dominance and submission, all featuring the face of the haughty friend; that face with its ironic gaze and air of disdain for the natural pleasures of life. I could imagine her doing all sorts of things then for men who pressed envelopes of cash into her hand and then wanted to use her as an object only. Yet I did not want only to imagine what she might have done. I wanted to know what she had done, and so I pressed Carina to tell me more.

'What happened?" I asked. "What made it so awful?" As I spoke, I was trying to keep the tone of fervent interest out of my voice, hoping that if I did so with sufficient success, then she might be lulled into telling me all of the details. It did not occur to me then that of course she had wanted to tell me; that she would not have introduced the topic had she not.

"Well, you absolutely mustn't repeat this to anyone else," she said, "but she had to go to an office in central London and there were two men there. At first they just asked her lots of questions; about her sex life and what she would be prepared to do with her clients. She said that she thought that was all it would be – questions. But then after a while they told her to take off her clothes, right there in front of them.'

"And she did?" I prompted hopefully, at the same time feeling myself growing strangely hot at the mental image that presented itself to me.

"She had to," Carina said, a mixture of awe and fear and something else in her voice. "And when she was completely naked, they took photos of her in all kinds of poses; on the couch and sitting on the desk and then down on her hands and knees on the floor. She said that while they were taking photos of her, she could see that they were both getting erections, but she didn't really think that that would mean anything, until they had finished taking photos and then they told her that she needed to show them what she was willing to do. She didn't want to at first, of course. She said that she didn't really trust them. But then they told her that any girl who worked for that agency had to do it, because if they wouldn't the agency could not trust that they would do it with clients and that would make them look bad and cost everyone money. She said it felt like they were making an effort to be kind to her and so eventually she told them that she would. They both got up and came around the desk and stood there leaning against it. Then they had her kneel in front of them and undo their trousers and start giving them each a blowjob, holding onto one with each hand and moving from one to another, sucking them for a minute or so before going on to the other. They got really excited, she said, and kept grabbing her head and forcing her to suck them deeper and deeper. With one that didn't really matter so much because she said that he was quite small. But the other was really big and every time he forced more down her throat, she was felt like she was going to choke on it. But she didn't try to stop them or say no, because she had already started by then and thought that she would be stupid not to go on and get it over with."

By this time, I remember feeling myself growing wet, and as I listened, I slid one hand under the sheet to begin touching myself through the silk of my French-knickers.

"Go on," I urged her, trying to keep any sound of what I was doing from my voice, "what happened then?"

"Well," she continued, her own voice a little husky, "the big one got behind her after a while and pulled her up so that she was standing, with the smaller one's cock still in her mouth. And then the big one slammed into her. She said that he didn't even touch her first to see if she was ready. He just thrust his whole cock inside her so that she felt like she was going to explode, and as soon as he was inside, he started going at it like there was no tomorrow, slamming into her so hard that the smaller one was completely in her mouth and his balls were slapping against her chin."

My fingers, had slipped under the fabric of my knickers by then and I began to rub my pussy, gently at first, then sliding first one then two fingers inside myself. I felt wetter than I had ever felt before.

"And then?"

"Well, the big one kept going at her," she said, "until the smaller one told him to switch places. So they did and apparently the big one made her stick her tongue out and he slapped his cock against it again and again, telling her what a good girl she was, what a slut. While he was doing that she wasn't really paying attention to what the other one was doing, but then she heard him spit a few times and suddenly she felt him pushing his cock against her… her other hole."

Her voice had begun to come out breathlessly, and I wondered if she too were aroused by what she was telling me. Yet she did not stop with her story, but went on telling it almost dreamily as though it left her mouth without her being conscious of it.

"She reached out to stop him, but he just batted her hand away and then shoved himself inside her, forcing her forward, so that she was almost choking again on the big one. She said it was a good thing the smaller one was smaller, because no one had ever done that to her before and she was sure that if he had been any bigger she would have cried and probably it would have felt like he were splitting her in two."

"Did she like it?"

'How can you ask that?" Carina demanded, yet it seemed to me that the husky desire in her voice overwhelmed the outraged tone she had intended to use. "But she couldn't stop it. Anyway, she said that they were both incredibly worked up by then and after about thirty seconds the man in her… in her arse, started coming, roaring like a wild animal as he did so. Then the big man put her down onto her knees again and had her open her mouth, and jacked himself off until he shot his… his sperm, all over her face and in her mouth and then, just when she was trying to subtly spit it out, he thrust his cock all the way into her mouth and had her lick it clean…"

She suddenly broke off from her story, but I hardly realised it at the time. I was shaking and writhing under my fingers and, not waiting to hear any more, I threw off the sheet and tearing my knickers aside, I took a long toy from my bedside table and having sucked it into my mouth, slid into my aching pussy, imagining as I did so that like her friend, I was giving myself to some faceless man in return for the opportunity to sell my body to whichever other man had the money to pay for it. I moaned and cried out, dropping the phone and clawing at the bedsheets, raising my pussy to meet my every thrust until suddenly, barely ten seconds later, I heard myself almost screaming out my orgasm, picturing that pretty, haughty, untouchable friend receiving the man's come shooting deep into her tight, unsullied arse in a seemingly endless stream. Vaguely, as the pleasure shook me, I heard my friend's shocked voice, calling my name from the phone on the bed beside me, but I paid her no mind.

# A RARE AND BEAUTIFUL ROSE

During the period in which Carina recounted the story of the young escort to me, I had long since left the banker and, after a series of fleeting encounters that do not merit mention here, had found myself with another man whose idea of me was at odds with the idea I had of myself. He was neither dull nor perfect on paper as the banker had been; though it is fair to say that he came near to perfection in looks. He was tall and well built, with black hair and very blue eyes. His face was handsome, his voice deep, and his manner confident to the point of arrogance. One of the things I liked about him was that he naively believed that he was incapable of being surprised by anything in the world; that he had experienced the world and knew it. He did not seem to particularly like the world as he had seen it. But he liked me; or rather he liked the idea of me that he had developed. He always called me his innocent, his rose. He said he wanted to treasure and protect me from all of the sordid wickedness of the world; from all its vice and depravity; the same vice and depravity that at the same time he admitted to seeking out not infrequently before knowing me. He said I had a goodness that shone out of my eyes; a rare, genuine goodness that was so vivid, so immediately recognisable that it hardly seemed possible that it was real. He told me that my movements were simple and innocent too, and my voice and laugh so sweet. When he spoke to me, he did so softly and without any of the vulgarities that littered the conversations I overheard that he had with his friends. When he made love to me, he did so gently, tenderly, saying when I asked him why he was so gentle, that he did not wish ever to soil me or dim that untouchable angelic quality that he said I had to me. He told me that my body, of all the bodies he had seen, was the most perfectly formed; he often described, in loving detail my "firm, upturned breasts below which a tapering waist gave way to a lushly rounded bottom, and warm, thick thighs that begged to be kissed and bitten and squeezed." Yet at the same time, he said that to him it was a body that seemed untouched; that it was impossible to image that others "had pawed and clawed at it"; that they had kissed and licked and massaged every inch of it. Impossible and painful to imagine, like the spoiling of a beautiful painting with graffiti, or the dumping of litter in a paradise garden. Any time, he said, he thought of it being used in a way that resembled anything other than tender worship, he said he had to fight to push the images from his mind, pretending that they could not be the case. And yet, he knew that they must have been. I was not so very young. I was in my twenties. I had lived in the world before he caught me smiling at him from the other side of the café in which we met. Yet to accept that they could have been, would have been to accept that he did not know me as he thought he did; that I was not as he imagined. Almost ceaselessly he looked for confirmation of the image he had of me, and seemed always to find it, though I did not understand how, in my movements, in my laugh that he said had such girlishness to it, in my smiles and words, in my occasional delight at the smallest of things – the taste of cake or the sight of a kitten gambling in the winter sunshine. He chose to see none of the wordly experience that he feared to see; no signs that I had been used as he had often used other young women; or worse, that, like those other young women, I had wanted to be used, to give and be given those pleasures of which innocence knows nothing. He said he did not know why that appearance of innocence was so important to him in me when it had never been before in anyone else. Perhaps it was that it inspired him to be better, he said, a little pretentiously, to be kinder and more selfless and thoughtful than he had ever shown signs of being, in order to be worthy of me. Perhaps, he admitted, it was some darker, more patriarchal desire to be with someone who had not given themselves to the pleasures of others, and enjoyed doing so. Whatever his motivation for looking for it, however, he did look and see it for three long months with me, until one night in early summer.

It was late that night. The lights were off and the room was lit only by the faint orange glow from the street lights, which crept in through a crack in the shutters along with the warm, night air. He was half asleep, lying on his side with my small body pressed against his back. He told me later that he had assumed I was sleeping too, but then he felt my hand slide from his hip, up and under the waistband of his boxer shorts down to his crotch. At the touch of my fingers, his cock began to stir. Never before had I touched him uninitiated by kisses and caresses on his part. I had wanted, I think, to play the part that he had cast for me. I had enjoyed appearing to be innocent whilst knowing the real desires that flowed through me, and the things that I did when I was not with him; the strangers from the dimly lit bars, and the friends from home who sometimes came out to visit me. Yet by that night I had grown tired of the double life. I was not innocent, and I had tired of the pretence of being so, though it had amused me for a time. I began gently to stroke up and down, causing him grow thick and hard in my hand. He stifled a moan, as though not wishing to scare me off, yet still rolled onto his back. I pushed the covers back over him and on my knees beside him, pulled his boxer shorts down, bent over and took him in my mouth.

The moan that escaped him then seemed one that was only half of pleasure, half of surprise. Just as I had never touched him uncued before, I had never taken him in my mouth. Looking back, I do not know why. I had wanted to, yet it had seemed that doing so might ruin the game of pretend that I was playing; might stop him looking on me as an angel, and see me for what I really was. And he had never asked me to. As my tongue moved slowly, sliding wetly up the underside of his cock, then swirling around the tip before sliding back down, all the time exerting a pressure which held him against the roof of my mouth, he must have realised that though I had never pleasured him in that way, it was not the first time I had given pleasure thus. I wondered if that thought, given his reaction to very idea of me having been with others, disturbed him, or heightened the thrill of pleasure that I was sure ran through him in that moment. And the thought that it might, gave me a thrill too, as did the feeling of him so hard and warm in my mouth, and the sound of his breathing, deep and ragged above me. One of my hands held him in place, not moving, but simply squeezing gently as my mouth gradually worked its way up and down, taking him deeper and deeper with every journey. When I touched his balls, I could feel them tightening and tasted a steady flow of pre-come across my tongue. I wondered whether he realised that too; and whether he knew, deep down, that as I was tasting it, I was recalling other times I had tasted that sweet, salty liquid; remembering how other men had felt in my mouth as I gave them pleasure. Now and then I would lift my head, sucking hard, and allow his cock to pop out from between my lips with a satisfying sound and I would glance up at him, relishing the blurred eyes, and look ecstasy on his face as jerked my hand up and down quickly, licking the head of his cock like a kitten licking up cream, before suddenly engulfing him once more in my mouth. He was groaning more deeply with every movement, I knew that he was feeling trembling waves of pleasure follow the movements of my lips while he watched me in the dim half-light. After a few minutes, pressed back against the pillow, he slid his hand between my legs and began running his middle finger over the folds of my pussy through my underwear. I moaned too then, sending fresh vibrations through him. Ever since I had begun to kiss down his chest, I had been aching to be touched. I lifted my head once more, reached behind me and swept the silken shorts I wore to bed down over my legs and dropped them onto the floor before resuming my position. My sex was wet and hot to the touch when fingertips had brushed over it in taking off my underwear, my little clit, an erect bump in the folds of my lips. He must have realised, perhaps with a jolt of shock, when he too touched me, that I was deeply aroused, powerfully aroused from being on my knees, sucking him deep into my mouth, by running my tongue all over him, by pleasuring him and tasting him. Perhaps then, he began to realise what I really was. Yet, if he did, it changed nothing in his actions. He toyed with me expertly, circling my clit gently, then running his finger from the soft skin behind my pussy up over me and back to the clit, pausing for only a fraction of a second each time, to slide his finger tip inside of me; with every moment heightening my arousal further. As my moans joined his own and the caresses of his fingers increased in fervour, so too did the passion of my sucking. He began to lengthen the strokes of his finger, beginning now over the opening of my anus, lingering there to run a few gentle circles before running to my pussy, transferring some of my flowing wetness there to lubricate me. After a minute or so, I pressed back against his finger, and in response he gently eased the tip into what I am sure he thought of as my tight, forbidden hole. I moaned louder, feeling a new pleasure throbbing through me. Slowly, he began to ease his finger in and out adding more and more lubrication until he was pressing knuckle deep in me, stretching me, and filling me in a way that only made me want more. Then suddenly, I could take no more and pushed his hand away and rose from from kneeling position.

"Do you have a condom?" I whispered, hearing something new, husky and full of desire sounding in my voice. Eagerly, still almost unbelievingly, he nodded and reached for the drawer and as he did so, he noticed me taking the tube of lubricant from the other drawer, and his eyes grew wide with shock. Perhaps he had thought that the tube of lubricant was a secret; a relic of his past before I had entered his life; something I would be dismayed by, or disgusted by. But that reaction of shock, only had the effect of making me more eager. I took the condom from him and pushed him back against the pillows. Then, having applied it, I squirted lube over of his cock, then over my fingers which I rubbed between the cheeks of my arse, over my anus, slipping first one finger, then two inside of me as I did so. And then I was straddling him, holding his prick at an upward angle as I slowly began to ease it inside my impossibly tight opening. The sensation was almost mind-blowing in its intensity. I felt the tip of his cock move through my ring and then deeper and deeper inside me, filling me completely and in a way that I had never felt filled before. I gasped and he did too. My tightness gripped him, smooth and silk-like, yet hard and strong, and bigger than he had ever seemed before, and yet, I seemed to stretch with ease to accommodate me. Slowly, slowly, I eased myself down on him until his whole length was inside me. Then I paused and glanced at him, momently, seeing his eyes wide and glazed with pleasure. Then I began rising and falling on his cock while he grasped my breasts in his hand and kneaded them, pinching the nipples lightly with first his fingers and then, leaning forward, between his lips and teeth, causing the pleasure that I felt below to rise up through the whole of my body. My moans turned to cries of pleasure, and I reached down to begin frantically rubbing my clit, and all the while driven almost mad by the feeling of him squeezed deliciously inside of me. Faster and faster I rose and fell, slamming myself against him while my fingers worked in ever increasing desperation. My cries rose in volume and at the same time, I felt him swelling as his own orgasm built to an uncontrollable climax, and I was coming and a second later he was coming too, shooting jet after jet of come into the condom inside of me. Our shared climax seemed to last an age, though it must have over in less than thirty seconds and I fell forward on top of him gasping.

    For several minutes we lay like that, breathing heavily, while his cock remained hard inside of him. Then gingerly I pushed myself up and very carefully slipped his cock out of me, dismounted him, and disappeared toward the bathroom, leaving him him, meanwhile, having taken off the condom and flung it into the bin, lying there, trembling, while his still-hard cock felt seemed to throb and twitch with a continuing pleasure.

"That was not," he said when I came back to bed, "the first time that you had done that. Nor the first time you had enjoyed it. Was it?"

"No," I told him with smile.

"No," he repeated. Then he sighed and looked deep into my eyes as if searching for something there before speaking again. "Yet," he went on, "it is strange; the idea does not cause me to want you less, or think less of you. Far from it. I thought I liked you so much because you were innocent. But now I see that the only thing more powerful than innocence, more attractive, is a facade of innocence beneath which the currents of desire run deep."

"Beware what you wish for," I told him. "I wonder if you truly want to know just how deep my desires run."

# THE PIANIST

In men, I have always looked for something that I do not myself possess. I look for arrogance, to contrast with the self-doubt I feel. I look for a slavish devotion, for a commitment to something, some work, or creative endeavour, because for my own part I find I can stick at things for so short a period of time before I become distracted or bored and move on to something else. I look for idealism, for a true, deep rooted belief in something, because I have none. I look for self-awareness, because I feel I know myself so little. I look for violence, for impulsiveness, for a force of character, for monogamy, for foresight. I want to find these qualities in the men I am with, and to reward them for them. Sometimes it works that way, but more often I have found them changing in the time we are together, which always causes me to feel a mixture guilt, at perhaps being at least partially responsible for their transformation, and disappointment bordering on disgust that the image they presented of themselves when we first met was not their true image, or at least not the image of the man they would always be. My deepest desire is to be with a man of genius; a man whom I can admire and worship and want to be submissive to, since I know that he will never feel inferior to me, or disappoint me. But such men as that are either all but impossible to find or, if you do find one, impossible to live with.

  I remember one man, who I met the winter I studied music in Italy, having left the man who thought me a rare and beautiful rose to seek out new experiences and pleasures on away from places where people knew me. The man I met was as pure a genius as anyone is likely to find. He was a pianist by profession, but there was hardly an instrument he could not play with skill of a virtuoso. He had only to take an instrument in his hands; hands which were long-fingered and delicate and beautiful as are those of all true artists; and suddenly whatever room he was in would grow still, breathless, and he would fill it with music of such beauty that you felt that you had been transported suddenly and completely to the gardens of Paradise. Violin or cello, piano or harp, you would feel the notes flow over you and through you, caressing you, raising you to a pitch of fury, or desire, or jealousy, or else bringing you low with sadness, heartbreak, with a profound awareness of every tragedy of life. He could make you weep with but a few notes, or cause that place between your legs to grow hot and wet, to throb with an almost overwhelming need to be touched. While he played, he was the master of all those who listened. He had the power to conduct, to move and command and control his audience in anyway he liked. Yet when he stopped, he became only a man again. A handsome man, it was true; tall and dignified, with velvety dark eyes and a tanned, rugged face and thick black hair only slightly tinted with grey about the temples. Yet, he was not exceptional. In his movements and figure, which though slim was not that of an athlete, he all but disappeared into the background, blurring in with the crowd. To the rest of his audience, perhaps that did not matter, but to me, it seemed a tragedy in itself. While he played, I was in the presence of a god. When he did not, the god disappeared and I felt frustrated and angry, desperate to be in that presence again.

I heard him play in the conservatoire ten, twelve, fifteen times, in the first few months I was there. Then I discovered by chance that he also gave private piano lessons in his house to those students who could afford the shockingly high prices he charged. I was delighted. The idea of having him play only for me, to sit beside him and watch his hands toy with the keys, move gently, expertly across them and draw from the instrument its ecstatic chorus, seemed to me the most wonderful of dreams.

I do not remember where I got the money from, but I did and I paid for six lessons. I remember going to his house the first day and being met by him at the door, dressed in shirtsleeves and elegantly cut black trousers, and being led by him up to the top of the house where there was a kind of conservatory on the roof, filled with deep Persian rugs and huge earthenware pots containing rose bushes and small fruit-trees, and in the centre of all, beneath the rushing clouds of the Venetian sky, a beautiful grand piano with a long, leather topped bench in front of it and a single lamp beside it, casting a faint orange glow over the keys.

He had me sit on the bench and sat down beside me, so close that I could feel his shirt sleeve brush against my bare arm whenever he shifted in his seat, and could feel the warmth of him and smell the faint fragrance of his aftershave mingling with the scents of the rose blossoms. He spoke softly to me, then placed some sheets of music before me and asked me to play. I did so, yet my fingers seemed alien to me. I could not make them move as they ordinarily would. I felt awkward and my playing was bad. Yet he listened patiently and only when I was finished did he tell me what I should have done, what I needed to improve. I heard his words, yet they did not go in. The soft voice, deep and musical, was pleasing to hear. What I wanted, however, was not to be spoken to, not to be taught, but to be played to. At last he gave me what I wanted. His left arm crossing in front of my body, almost touching my breasts, he began to play the piece of music by way of demonstration. The moment he began, the teacher – handsome, polite, and kindly – disappeared and the god returned. The music entered me, filled my soul, sent trembling pulses of pleasure running through me. It made me breathless; made my head seem to spin. It made me unconsciously press my thigh against his and lean forward just a little so that, as he moved his across the notes, his arm made contact, almost imperceptibly, with my breast. And then he stopped. I think I may have let out a moan of disappointment then, for I remember that he looked at me sharply, uncomprehendingly. However, he said nothing about it. He merely had me play the piece again, stopping me now and then to make suggestions, before having me start over. For all the good his coaching did, he might as well have stayed in silence, for my playing did not improve – far from it, it seemed only to get worse. I could sense his frustration as he told me again and again the same things. Yet his frustration was nothing to mine. I did not want to learn. I wanted only to listen. For the next forty-five minutes, however, despite me asking him twice to demonstrate again, he did not touch the piano, but merely directed me. I thought I should go mad for longing to hear him play. I wanted to feel the sensations of his music surge through my body, to feel my soul transported. And instead the man's voice, not the god's, instructed and corrected and scolded and droned.

Almost I had given up hope that I should hear him again, but at last, in the last ten minutes of the lesson, he took out another score, placed it on the piano and proceeded to play, having explained that this was the music we would work on in my next class. What ecstasy! The man disappeared and the god took his place once more, and all the pleasure that I had not found in the world, I found in his performance. For almost five blissful minutes, I sat and listened, pressing my body against his, thrilling with the passion, the sensuality of the sound. Then at last it was over and coming back to myself I felt him place the music in my hand and take my elbow to help me back to my feet. Downstairs at the front door, he smiled and gave me a small bow, then said; "Until next week then," and I left thinking all the while, "Next week? Next week? How shall I survive until next week."

I did survive of course and gradually I began to find ways of making him play more than merely a few minutes each class. I would bring him music and ask him how it should sound. Or I would play with such poor tempo or understanding of the sentiments of the piece, that he would at last grow annoyed and demonstrate for me. While the man was present, I felt nothing but frustration. Yet when he played and the god came out, I found myself to be falling in love with him. Love, perhaps, is not the right word. To be falling into a slavish devotion to him; an obsessive state of need for him, for his presence, for his music. I wanted him to play for me always. Yet as his student, I began to realise that I would never have that. And so I set out to seduce him. I wore loose silk blouses with nothing underneath, unbuttoned sufficiently that when I leaned forward he could not escape catching a glimpse of my naked breasts. I wore heels and pencil skirts with splits that revealed my thighs. I wore perfumes the scent of which was created to seduce. I brushed against him, and leaned my shoulder against his. Accidentally I dropped a pencil or a sheet of music that fell on the other side of him, and before he could rescue it, I leaned over him and picked it up, making sure to press my breasts against his lap, or brush my hair lightly across his chest. I smiled inviting smiles at him. I lowered my eyes submissively. I stretched so that the fabric of my shirts would cling to the curves of my body. And as I listened I took to placing the tip of my finger between my lips, as though in thought, lightly sucking it as I listened to him. All taken together, he could not help but notice these things. Yet he did not seem certain as to how to react. I felt that he was wondering still whether they were accidental, or whether I were simply one of those women who delight in tempting only so long as the temptation is not given in to. Gradually, however, he seemed to gain in confidence. He smiled and laughed more and complimented me. Yet this was not what I wanted. Then at last he kissed me; a soft, beautiful kiss, yet even so the kiss only of a man. I kissed him back, opening my lips beneath his and teasing him with my tongue and I felt his arms close around me, pressing my body against his and I knew then that I had won. His hands wanted to explore my body, to squeeze and caress my breasts, to pinch my nipples, or ease apart my thighs and toy with what he found between, but I would not let him. I pushed him from me, and having rubbed his hardening cock through his trousers, I gently undid the flies and took it out. I looked deep into his eyes, and then commanded – not asked, nor requested, nor begged, but commanded – him to play for me. He looked surprised, taken aback, and began to say something, but I merely put a finger to his lips.

"Play for me," I told him, "and I will give you pleasure. Stop, and I will stop."

And then I lowered my head into his lap and took his hard cock deep into my mouth. For a moment I heard nothing but a deep groan of pleasure, and I remained immobile. Then I felt his arms brush passed my head, and he began to play. The music filled the room, swirling about it, seeming to fill every particle of the air and every particle of my being with pleasure and joy. Almost I could do nothing but listen. Yet I remembered what I had promised and, the music filling my soul, I began to pleasure him, to tease and stimulate him, to drive him wild with the ministrations of my lips and tongue. I sucked him deep into my mouth, tasting him, feeling him throb against my throat, and then rose and flickered my tongue across the smooth head of his cock until he was trembling and thrusting upward toward me, and then I took him deep into my mouth again. Once, he groaned and the music faded, but immediately I stopped too and, after a moment or two, clearly desperate to feel more, he began to play again. Slowly I pleasured him, drawing back whenever I felt his orgasm was too close, and then intensifying my attentions once more, all the while myself being sent into raptures by his music. At last, twenty minutes or more after we had begun, he came to the climax of a piece and its crescendo so filled me with passion that I sucked almost desperately at him, driving him as deep as I could, burying my head in his lap, until, with the last notes of the piece, I felt him tense and fill my mouth with his come. The music ended and he slumped back on the stool, exhausted and sated and human once more. I placed him back inside his trousers and did them up and then rose to leave. Before I went to the door, however, I smiled at him.

"I do not want any more lessons," I told him. "I want to come here when I choose and listen to you play. If you do that, if you play like you just did, I will pleasure you like I just did. What do you say?"

He looked at me through bliss-blurred eyes and nodded almost weakly.

"Whatever you want," he said.

And so I left that day, but not for the last time. Again and again I went back, and made him play for me, pleasuring him only so long as he played. We went on like that for months. Mostly I would pleasure him with my mouth, but sometimes, when the music he played roused me to a state of near mania, I would place myself in his lap, with my legs wrapped around him, and ride him until we came together to the crescendo of the music. At last, it came to an end only because he wanted more from me than simply pleasure, and refused to play until I promised to give it to him. I could not; for when he was not playing, he was no more worthy of sacrificing my freedom to than any other of ten thousand men. Yet, I remember the music and what it did to me, and I dream that one day I will find another genius, albeit one who will not cease to be special the moment they are not employed in their art.

# MAD AS BIRDS

Following my obsession with the pianist, I lingered on in Italy, though I ceased to study music. It was beautiful time, filled with new people and new adventures. Though none lasted long, I felt that I was learning something from each of them; if was as if in direct correlation with my process of freeing my passions, my curiosity and desire for knowledge grew, and always the two things walked hand in hand. I remember one or two incidents in particular where this can be most clearly seen. I was sitting in a café in a new lover's home town, where he had brought me for the weekend. The sky above was a deep blue, in which the first stars had begun to appear between the shadowy Cypress trees, and the evening about us was warm and seeming to throb with a life more vibrant than I had ever known. It infected me, thrilled me; the sound of the guitars playing their haunting melodies, and the music of the voices, sensual and deep, and the dusty earth beneath our table, and the scents of food and wine and orange blossom. It seemed to cause the life to course through my veins with a sensuous, electric power. Everywhere there were people hurrying passed, it seemed to me, towards their own passionate, mysterious night-time adventures. And the people were so beautiful; all dark, with glossy black hair; the men so lithe and handsome, so brooding; the women all proud and sultry, dressed in summer clothes that seemed to cling to their tanned, shapely bodies, as silken sheets caress naked lovers in the throws of their ecstasy.

  While we drank our wine, my eyes flickered over everything, drinking it all in, while beside me, my lover sat watching me and the crowd with a knowing smile playing across his lips. Then quite suddenly a young woman on her own passed us and I sensed rather than saw my lover look at the young woman and then turn away, shielding his face behind one deeply tanned hand. I glanced at the him, then turned back to look as the young woman sat down at the café opposite and called the waiter to bring her a vermouth. When I looked again at my lover, I saw the smile was gone, and a faint colour had suffused his cheeks.

"Who is she?" I remember asking, half-afraid, half-eager to have him confirm what I felt I already knew; that here was a woman from his past; a past about which he spoke so little.

"Someone I used to know," he said, letting his hand fall, but shifting in his seat as he did so, so that his face would not be visible to the young woman at the other café.

"An old lover?" I asked, feeling a need to make him tell me explicitly, though not from jealousy. To my surprise, I wanted then to know because a part of me felt a strange, powerful desire to imagine the young woman *with* him; the two of them together as they must once have been.

"Perhaps," he said. That was all. It was of course a confirmation, yet it was not enough to satisfy me.

"She is very beautiful," I prompted, my urge to hear more quickening at his unwillingness to share.

He shrugged.

"Beautiful and as mad as birds."

"And is that why you left her?"

He looked at me and when his eyes met mine I saw no shame in them, but something else; not sadness, nor regret nor longing; only memory.

"Of course. What else should I have done?"

I turned from him to look at the woman once more, taking in the bright, pretty face, perhaps a little too heavily made up, and the shining dark hair and startlingly blue eyes, and then her body, the slender waist and long legs and the heavy, full breasts half revealed by the silk shirt she wore open down to the fourth button. She did not look mad. She looked confident and happy. Yet perhaps, there was a hint of danger in that happiness. It seemed so wild and unrestrained, caused by nothing but the words of the waiter as he put down the drink in front of her.

"Some people say," I said, turning back to him, "that the mad ones make better lovers. Is it true?"

He shrugged once more.

"That depends on the form of madness, I suppose. And, on how you define *better*."

"And in her case?"

"There were few things she would not do," he said, his voice betraying no emotion. "If one wanted one's life to be a pornographic film, then she would be one's ideal partner. But for me, I cannot live on lust alone."

I looked back at the girl and felt the strange tremor of excitement running through me deepen. I wanted then to picture the young woman doing all of those things that the innocent delight in her face made it almost impossible to believe that she was capable of, yet I could not. I needed him to give me images that I knew to be true, or else all I would have would be a vague blur that had no more truth to it than the images we create of all strangers who excite our interest in one way or another.

"Tell me what she was like," I said, without changing the direction of my gaze. "What did she use to do to you?"

I heard him let out a soft, derisive snort, but still did not turn back to him.

"She would lose her mind over the smallest thing," he said. "She would threaten me and berate me if she did not feel that she was the centre of my world. She would seek out my former girlfriends and warn them to stay away from me, though they had shown no interest in reconnecting with me. She would disappear for days at a time and be found wandering in the countryside. She would burn the drafts of stories I wrote, because she thought that the female characters were some other woman I cared for. She would become violent at the drop of a hat, and then spend days begging forgiveness and threatening to hurt herself, only to be violent again. She was mad, that is all."

I remember shaking my head and trying to keep the frustration I felt out of my voice.

"But *that* was not what I meant. What was she like to be with, sexually?" I felt myself blush as the words left my mouth. Yet I wanted to know; wanted to picture it. "Was she very adventurous?"

He laughed again and I felt him shift in his seat.

"She was adventurous, of course," he told me, "but with a kind of desperation. There were so many things she used to all but beg me to do. She begged me to let her pleasure me every day; to let her ride my face until she came and then ride my hard cock until I came inside her. She begged me to rub her pussy through her panties in some public place, teasing her, making her steadily wetter and wetter until my fingers reached inside her panties and my first touch made her come. She begged me to let her kiss and lick down my stomach and then to undo my jeans and run her tongue all over my balls and caress them in her mouth before settling to kiss her *favourite cock* for hours." He accentuated the words *favourite* and *cock* as though they were direct quotes, changing the tone of his voice mockingly as he did. "She said she could hardly sleep for the desire to be licking and sucking it until she could taste my *sweet come* exploding all over her tongue. Is that the sort of thing you want to hear?"

I felt a sudden shortness of breath, a tightness in my stomach, but I nodded, my eyes running over and over the young woman's body and face as the images his words created began to run through my mind.

"Yes," I said, hearing a strange huskiness in my voice. "Go on."

"She begged me to come all over her breasts," he continued, his own voice seeming thicker and more urgent as all of the passion and pain he had felt for the woman arose in him again through the recollection of her, "in her mouth, in her hot, wet pussy, all over her face. She begged me to bend her over the bannister, over my desk, over her car bonnet, and thrust my cock deep inside her and fuck her until we came together in an earth-shattering shared climax. She begged me to kiss and lick her breasts while she touched herself. She begged me to eat meals off her naked body, to put my face between her breasts while she touched herself. She begged me to let her place her hand on the *huge bulge* in my lap and slowly undo my trousers to reveal my *magnificent, huge, delectable, one of a kind, spectacular cock* and then for me to fuck her from behind until her come was flowing from her and she was biting her lip, screaming my name. She begged me to tie her up and fuck her in the arse; and she begged me, after I was done fucking her, to let her *suck my sensitive, throbbing cock clean of come*. She told me that if only I would let her, she would pleasure me whenever I wanted, any moment of the day or night; that at a word from me she would drop her clothes and drop to her knees, ready to fulfil any desire I could imagine, whether we were alone or in the midst of a crowd. There was nothing I could not have done to her and few things that I did not do."

"I wager you still think about her," I said, feeling almost uncomfortably aware that in that moment I desperately wanted him to say that he did. I felt a wild desire then to get him to bring the young woman over to take a drink with us and then convince her to come back to our hotel, to do all of those things he had described, while I watched and participated beside her. She was so beautiful in the evening light; so fresh-looking and yet with an almost palpable sensuality about her. It was an impossible desire, of course, yet I felt it.

"I think of her as much as anyone thinks of their former lovers, I suppose," I heard him say, distantly. "Men especially never forget the erotic encounters they have enjoyed."

His tone calmed my imaginings a moment and I turned back to him, surprised almost to see that there was a sadness then in his eyes.

"Yet," I said, gently, "she was mad?"

"She was mad in the truest sense of the word," he said.

"And so you left her?"

"For my own survival I had to. Despite her desire to offer her body up to me to use in any way I saw fit, like the body of a slave in an eastern harem, in the end I ran away and abandoned her to others to enjoy. It was that or enslave myself to her emotionally, as she was willing to do for me physically. The price was not worth paying."

I sighed then and turned to take one more glance at the young woman, who had by then finished her drink and was calling the waiter back to settle for it.

"And yet," I said, thinking about the boldness, the willingness of the woman to give herself to someone so completely, "at least you had the experience of someone who was willing to fulfil your darkest fantasy. Not everyone has."

"Perhaps that is a good thing," he replied. "Fantasies when they are lived out, are sometimes dangerous things."

I thought for a moment and shrugged.

"It can be just as dangerous not to live them out," I said. "They torment you, haunt you, obsess you."

He looked at me then, and his expression changed. It was as though a faint spark of light had ignited in the deepest depths of his dark eyes.

"What fantasies obsess you?" he asked.

I remember smiling and telling him that I would tell him them all, later, whilst a voice inside me added; "Later, if I believe you are willing to help me fulfil them." By that time, you see, already I had begun to consciously look for partners who would do more than merely tantalise my desires. I had begun to look for those who would indulge them, even share them.

# WHAT IT WAS LIKE FOR HIM

After my lover had told me of the girl who was as mad as birds, I found myself strangely obsessed with hearing how men felt in making love, in fucking – what the sensation was truly like for them. And so it was that he told the story, because I asked him to, one afternoon when we were lying naked on my bed with the winter sunlight streaming in through the windows. I had wanted for some time to understand why it was that he was so obsessed with my mouth and took more pleasure from it than he seemed to take from any other part of me; why indeed so many men seemed to do the same. I liked to give pleasure in that way, I always had, sensing the power I held over my lover as I did so. Yet, I wanted to understand more; to know what it was like for him; to know what sensations a man felt in his bliss. So, believing that our tastes and desires are often defined by our earliest experience, I asked him to tell me about the first time a woman had pleasured him in that way. And he told me. He told me that the first time it had happened he had been a teenager with a girl a few months younger than himself. They had been at a party in the old stables of a farm in the country side, which had been converted into a sort of little house with a loft on which a dozen or so mattresses and duvets and a mountain of pillows had been laid out. When the party had passed its peak, all of those who were staying went up to the loft and settled down alone or with a partner, and someone had turned the lights low and they had all spoken in whispers to one another. He had been with the girl whose birthday they had been celebrating. While the others whispered, or amused each other in the shadows, the pair had kissed and explored each others bodies. He had sucked on her pert, rosebud nipples and had run his fingers over her mound and wet, waiting pussy until she squirmed beneath him and let out little moans of pleasure that he suspected those around them could not help but hear. Then he had told her to go down on him and without hesitation she had, worming her way beneath the duvet and taking his hard cock in her mouth. She had licked him all over, sucked him with inexpert enthusiasm for some minutes until one of her friends, glancing over in their direction, had asked where she was. Brief though it had been, the attention she had relished on him had been nothing like he had ever known before, he said. The feeling of her tongue on him, of her mouth – so warm and delicate; the feel of her hair brushing lightly across his stomach; the feeling of intense intimacy, of knowing that his cock was in her mouth; and the feeling of power – that he had told her to do so and she had obliged – all rushed through him at once. Yet the interruption of the moment by that friend's voice had tainted all of the new pleasures he had felt with frustration. She had stopped moving suddenly and then came up and lay beside him on the pillow, blushing, while her friends giggled around them. Later, when the attention of the others had been diverted elsewhere, she had been too nervous to continue and so, unable to restrain himself yet unable to recapture what he had had, he had had to finish himself off and had been left thoroughly dissatisfied.

I was disappointed by that story. It left me as unsatisfied as I imagined he had been in the moment of its happening. It had hinted at something, yet fully had explained nothing; had allowed me to understand little more than I had understood before. There had not been the enlightenment in it I had imagined I would find. Rolling over, therefore, so that I was lying with my head on his chest and my legs entwined with his, I asked him instead to tell me about the first time he had really enjoyed it. Perhaps, I thought, therein the true secret might lie; something of those hidden things that it was rarely given to the giver of pleasure to understand.

He had been eighteen that time and the girl with him might have been eighteen too but was already engaged to a someone much older. They had drunk together through an evening, and had flirted and exchanged caresses under the table. His car had been parked in one of the quiet streets behind the car-park of the bar in which they had been drinking, he recounted softly, running his fingertips lightly up and down my thighs as he did so, while for my part I saw that his sex was thickening and growing hard at the recollection. The street lamps there had made it easy to see, yet there had been no-one around and so they had got into the back of the car and pushed the front seats as far forward as they would go and had begun kissing without bothering to drive somewhere more secluded. On his side there had been a sense of urgency to the whole encounter. The fact that she was engaged and claimed to love her fiancé had made him feel that he had perhaps that opportunity only, that moment of madness on her part, to enjoy her, and he had not wanted to let the opportunity slip away into the night and memory. Her kisses had been hot and wet and eager and her arms were firm about him, holding him tightly, as though she were afraid that at any moment, he might stop. Having run his hands through her hair and traced the contours of her back through her clothes, he had reached under her jumper and begun massaging, gently at first, then with growing eagerness, the heavy breasts contained within the sheer silk of her bra. She had moaned a little then and drawn back to look at him with dark, liquid eyes, which seemed to have grown larger and become possessed by a hunger he had not seen in them before. Taking this to be a good sign, inexpert though he admitted he had been, he had pulled down her bra and begun kneading the large brown nipples beneath. They had come awake at his touch, hardening and pouting up at him. He had lowered his head to kiss and suck at them, teasing first one then the other with the lightest touch of his teeth. Her breathing had become heavy. She had thrust her breasts upwards, taking hold of his head at the same time to keep him in place. Then he had begun running his hand up her thigh under her skirt and soon his fingertips had touched the hot folds of her pussy through her panties. She had reached down and pushed his hand away. He reached again but that second time she had closed her legs, and jerked his head upward. He had thought she was going to put an end to it all then, but instead she had merely held him away from her, looking searchingly into his eyes for several long moments, and then she had begun once more to kiss him, more urgently this time, with a tongue that thrust its way into his mouth. He had reached for her breasts once more, but again she pushed his hand away. This time, however, she had reached with her own hand for his crotch, where his cock was straining against the fabric of his jeans. She had traced its outline with her fingertips, then very slowly had undone his belt and flies and reached in to pull it out. Her hand had been cold against him, he recalled, but it warmed quickly as she gently moved it up and down sending tantalising pulses of pleasure through him. He had leaned back and drawn her towards him to kiss her once more, but in that moment, remembering something she had told him about the delights to which she treated her fiancé, he had reached up to run his hand under her hair, then gently taken hold of her and guided her unresisting head down into his lap.

Her large, pouting lips had closed over the tip of his cock and he had felt her tongue begin to caress him, a sensation so rich that he had let out an involuntary gasp the moment he felt it. Then slowly, she had moved further and further down, massaging every part of him as his cock edged deeper into her mouth until it touched her throat.
"My God," he told me, "it was almost too much to bear and I had to fight the urge to come right there and then."

She had stayed like that a moment, he said, and then had begun to move her mouth up and down, never ceasing even for a moment the manipulations of her tongue as she did so, every moment giving him pleasure he had never previously imagined. He had felt like a prince being brought into a state of bliss by a beautiful courtesan; like a master being served ecstasy by a slave girl. And he had wanted, desperately wanted, for the sensation to go on forever. He had reached under her arm and taken one of her breasts in his hand once more, playing with the engorged nipple as he had felt his pleasure rising and rising, driving all other sensations and thoughts from mind and body. Once he reached again between her legs, but she had raised her head a moment and told him simple *'no'* before returning her mouth to its task. Even that moment of deprivation had felt like it were going to drive him mad, he remembered. Yet after it, the pleasure had continued to mount, moment by moment, consuming him, devouring him, hypnotising him, until he had found himself squirming in the seat, feeling his balls swell and strain and then finally, hissing a warning between his teeth, he had found he could hold back no longer and began exploding jet after jet of hot sperm into her willing mouth. She had seemed to suck harder as he came, bobbing her head slowly, exquisitely, until finally the torrent had ceased, and then she had raised her head a centimetre and swallowed before licking every drop which had escaped her from his trembling shaft and finally raising her head to be kissed. He had tasted the sperm on her tongue and lips, faintly sweet and salty at the same time. Then had he slumped back in his seat, his softening prick cradled in her hand and her head on his chest. Outside, a couple had passed by the window, but neither looked in, and he had been barely conscious of them so powerfully had the bliss she had given him affected him. For several minutes on end, he said, not a single thought crossed his mind. He had been aware only of the feeling that every molecule of his being was luxuriously, frenziedly stimulated and alive.

When finally he had recovered a little, they had begun to kiss again, as passionately as before and, this time, when his hand stroked up her thigh she had let him reach inside her panties where her pussy was hot and wet, its lips open to receive his fingers. He had played with her, teased her, and finally eased his middle finger deep inside her while his thumb circled her swollen clit. She had ground herself hard against him and began to buck and moan, biting at his neck, until finally she grabbed his arm and had held it still until the waves of her orgasm had passed. He had been aroused himself again by then, he said, and his cock was harder even than before. He had tried to ease her head back into his lap, desperate to feel again that magical caress of lips and tongue, but this time, she had resisted, taking his cock in her hand instead and stroking it vigorously until finally another orgasm took him, sending another series of jets of sperm over her hand and wrist and his trousers and the front of his shirt. Zipping himself up, he had watched her lick the sperm from her hand and wrist, then, wondering at the tantalising intimacy of the gesture, he had kissed her again and driven her back to where her own car was parked a few hundred yards away. They had not seen each other again for six months and then only briefly at her wedding reception. Yet still, the memory, he said, had stayed with him ever afterwards, and against it all other similar experiences were measured. Always, when he watched a woman kiss slowly down his chest and stomach, his body had come alive in a way that nothing else caused it to do, desperate to be transported back to that paradise to which the young woman in the lamp lit street had transported him.

  I did not know what, if anything, the story had taught me when he was done telling it. Yet I felt I knew, that I understood, at least something of what it truly meant for a man. It had aroused me too and awakened within me a sudden desire to give as maddening a pleasure as that young woman had given and so, gently, having kissed him lightly on the lips, I began to kiss down his chest and the defined abdominals below, making for the hard, smooth cock that seemed to tremble in anticipation of the touch of my lips, wondering as I did if I too would give him something he would recall so vividly in years to come.

# THE QUIET WOMAN

Beauty takes many forms and there have been times, many times, when masculine beauty was not that which entranced me most powerfully. At certain points in my life I have tired of it; found that it did not move me, as it did at other times. Yet I have never ceased to be fascinated by feminine beauty. In a man, beauty, if it exists, is usually simple; a complete harmony of physical qualities and behaviour all acting together as a whole. The slightest flaw causes it to disappear. In women, beauty is more complex. Often, in my experience, the impression of beauty is created by a single aspect of a woman and from that aspect beauty appears to spread outward through every part of them, rendering them beautiful in their entirety. Sometimes such beauty comes from a smile. Sometimes from a lovely pair of eyes. Sometimes from an attitude, or a form of movement, or a sentiment of goodness or happiness which reveals itself in a single expression. Sometimes it is the curve of a body from which beauty spreads, sometimes a tone of skin, or a river of glossy hair that catches the light and seems to shine like silk. Yet were that aspect removed and not replaced by something else, so too would the beauty it had brought to light disappear. Less often, beauty comes from several sources in the same person, all working together to increase the impression of overall beauty. If one of these aspects were to disappear, unlike a man, the woman would remain beautiful, though changed. Most rarely of all, all aspects of a person are beautiful. This last beauty, so uncommon, so unusual, is almost impossible to believe, or accept in its reality. I think in all my life, I have seen beauty like that less than a dozen times and only once that I can remember clearly. The others blend together in my mind as the memories of beautiful landscapes blend together, or of fine churches, or exquisite wines or cakes. That single perfect beauty, which alone I remember so clearly, remains clear because of what followed my first seeing it.

I glimpsed her first sitting at a table by the window of a Parisian café, not long after I left Italy, with a coffee in front of her and a book in her hand. I had just come in from a chilly, overcast November day. Yet when I glanced at her she appeared as if bathed in the warm amber light of a summer's evening. She was facing away from me, when I first looked at her. All I saw was a mass of shining black hair, tumbling in soft waves over slender, perfectly tanned shoulders. I took my normal seat at the counter and the waiter brought me coffee. I remember that I took a sip of the coffee and looked at her once more, and that that time she had turned slightly so that her face was visible to me, and that I froze, as though transfixed by what I saw.

No words will ever be adequate to describe the beauty of that woman, who appears to me still in my dreams as something like a dark, untouchable princess. So much of her beauty came from subtle, almost imperceptible qualities which combined together to make for that vision of other-wordly beauty I was struck by. Let it suffice to say that to me, as I imagined to many others, she was perfect. She had a smile that was shy and gentle, yet which seemed to light the whole world around her, even though in that moment it was only directed at something on the pages of the book she read, and which would have brought joy to even the most broken of hearts. Her eyes were a velvet brown, and soft, with a strange light in their depths, like the twinkling of a star half-veiled by night mist. Her skin was flawless and silken smooth, and seemed almost to glow with health and vitality. She had dimples and a delicate beauty mark at the corner of her mouth, and her lashes were long and luxuriant and untouched by mascara. In fact she seemed to me to wear no make-up at all, and perhaps that was because any would have been superfluous. Most striking of all was an angelic quality that clung to her, but one combined with an aura of strength, of self-reliance, of incorruptibility; as though she would be incapable of doing an awkward thing or saying a vulgar word or of doing anything at all that her heart did not lead her judge to be right. Her figure was cloaked in a loose jumper, cut to leave her shoulders bare, yet not clingy or tight, and a long skirt, yet what could be made out of its curves, only added to the vision of perfection she created. How I would have loved to be like her; to be her; to be with her.

Having once begun to look at her, I could not bring myself to look away. Neither, I noticed from out the corner of my eye could the waiter, who was an old friend of mine.
"A man," he said, leaning close to me over the counter, "would sell his soul for a woman like that without giving it a second thought."
"A woman too," I replied, without turning my gaze from the vision before me. "Yet, if you or I sold our souls, I doubt that they would go for much. Maybe enough for a smile, but nothing more."
"A smile is free for everyone," he told me. "You will see. She smiles at everyone. But more than that, no. In our dreams alone."

I did not doubt for a moment what he said. I thought then that few men or women would dare even to approach her. Her beauty, her air of reserve and of goodness, was too breathtaking to dream of being with her, of being close to her, of kissing or caressing her. Any such thing would have seemed like the basest sacrilege if done by any who was not as perfect as she, and none such could ever be imagined. I found myself wondering absently what her life must be. A beautiful life, quiet and unmarred by those things that always sullied the lives of those less beautiful than she.

She got up after a few more minutes, in which the waiter and I stared yearningly, hopelessly at her, and smiled at the waiter and walked, or rather seemed to float, out of the cafe and into the grey November afternoon, leaving only the most subtle hint of perfume behind her.

I went to café every afternoon of that week, hoping to see her, but she did not come back. I wondered many times where I might find her – not to speak to her or approach her, but just to look at her; to be in her presence again. Yet, I could not happen upon the answer. Several times I went to the bookshops along that street and those nearby and wandered between the shelves in the hopes of coming across her, yet she never appeared. I went also to the other cafés and to the cake shops and to all the places I imagined that the woman I dreamed her to be might go, but did not find her in any of those places either. Perhaps, I mused, I had imagined her. Perhaps the waiter had too. Perhaps her presence in the café had been form of collective fantasy. Or the visitation of a genuine angel. It was only at the end of the week that I discovered that I had simply been looking for her in all of the wrong places; that she had in fact been so close to where I had walked that I might have seen her every evening had I chosen.

The Friday of that week an old friend came to visit me in the city. He had done well, in whatever he was doing and wanted to throw his money around, so after dinner, which we ate in an expensive, rather pretentious restaurant, he took me to a high class burlesque show, the tickets of which cost more than I spent in a fortnight at the time. When we walked through the door, he asked rather grandly for the best box in the house but was told that it was taken, and was offered another smaller box in the upper tier and complained about it all the way up there. For my part, arriving in the little box, I felt like a duchess. It was very small, with just enough space for the two of us, but it was high up, with a magnificent view of the stage and of the crowd below and of what must have been the best box, a very grand affair with a woman and two men sitting in it, across from ours.

We had arrived just in time, and even as we took our seats the show began. In front of us, the lights dimmed and a single spot was turned on, illuminating a space high above the stage in a warm, red light. For a moment there was silence. Then in the background, faintly at first, the deep strains of a cello began to sound. As the music swelled, the circle of light grew and then split in two, each travelling out from the centre to reveal two platforms, one on either side of the stage. And there on each, a beautiful devil stood with a trapeze in her hands. One devil was black as night, the other blonde, both in black silken leotards that accentuated every curve of their figures, with long black tails, and red horns emerging from their hair, which was swept back in high ponytails. For a time, these devils danced, swaying in time with the music, their arms and legs performing beautifully gymnastic manoeuvres that further stretched their outfits over their wonderful bodies. Then, quite suddenly the heads of both figures snapped toward the space between them. A third light, this one white, had come on there and as the crowd followed the looks of the devils, into the white light, standing on a third trapeze, swung a woman; the most beautiful of all women, dressed in nothing but strips of red silk. She swung into the light and, to either side, the two figures leaned far out from their platforms, supporting themselves with one hand gripped on their trapezes, their heads following her every movement, their free hands reaching out toward her. As the third figure swung, I felt my chest tighten with excitement and nervousness. There, her glossy black hair flowing behind her, her perfect neck arched, and her beautiful eyes raised to the ceiling, was my dark princess of the café. I could hardly believe it, yet it was true. Still angelic, and strong, and untouchable, yet transported to new heights of beauty, there could be no mistaking her.

As she swung by, one of the devils reached out to the furthest extent of her arm and made a grab at the figure in red, but succeeded only in catching hold of a corner of one of the silks before the woman had swept away back into the white light. The devil kept hold of the silk and it came away from the woman's body with an almost audible swish, revealing just a hint of golden skin. The other devil, apparently driven into a frenzy of desire by this, leapt from her own platform and swung her own trapeze passed the woman in red, slipping down on her trapeze in mid air, gripping it behind her knees to leave both hands free, and reaching for the woman herself. My dark princess, however, leapt high to avoid the grasping hands, caught the trapeze again with a grace and expertise that caused the crowd to erupt in applause, and swung away.

Her evasion, however, brought her back in the direction of the black devil, who in turn launched herself from the platform and there, high above the stage, succeeded in catching the corner of a second silk and stripping it from the my dark princess. Again and again the performance was repeated. Sometimes the dark princess would evade her attackers and swing lightly by leaving them grasping at thin air; while at other times, one or the other, through some cunning acrobatics, would succeed in stripping another silk from her. The performance finally came to a climax, when at last my dark princess was dressed only in a single ribbon of red silk that snaked across her breasts and between her legs. Returning to her platform, she stood for a moment, looking from one devil to the other, and then suddenly stripped the silk from herself and cast it down between them, revealing a body so perfect it took the breath away. The music swelled and the woman raised her arms and seemed to cast herself after the ribbon into thin air, twisting even as she fell. For a moment it seemed she would fall to her death on the stage far below. The two devils, however, had anticipated her act and swung toward her and at the very last moment, they caught her as she fell, one by her ankles the other by her wrists. They held her, all three suspended in the air between their two trapezes, and turned her over and over, revealing to the audience now breasts, now her perfect rear and smooth back, and the dark shadow of her sex. As they turned her, the trapezes were lowered and came smoothly down to the stage, where the two devils instantly fell upon the woman, kissing all over her body. Then, just as quickly, they were up on their feet, and they had lifted her between them and raised her above their heads and carried her off through the black curtains at the back of the stage.

My friend sat for a minute in silence as the crowd applauded wildly around us, his eyes fixed on the place where my dark princess had disappeared. Then, shaking his head slowly, he let out a long, low whistle.

"Have you ever seen so beautiful a woman?"

I did not even bother to reply. I was too busy thinking to myself, cursing to myself, that for a second time the gods had smiled on me and let me see her, but that undoubtedly they would not do so again. I was thinking too, about the transformation I had seen in her; from the daytime's gentle beauty, to this powerfully erotic temptress of the night. It was of course the same woman, but transformed from an angel into a goddess it seemed to me.

"Want to go downstairs and see if we can see her in her dressing room?" my friend asked. "For a few notes, they might let us."

"They won't," I told him. "If I worked here, I wouldn't. I wouldn't let anyone near her. And anyway, there'll be a mass of people trying."

"Suit yourself," he said, getting up. "But I am going to try."

And with that he turned and went out of the box, leaving me staring blankly down at the crowd below, as a new show began on the stage. I felt like something had been torn from me then. And I felt too, a surge of anger and disgust that my friend had seen her, yet had not recognised in her that seemingly impossible manifestation of perfection that should have kept him from even thinking of trying to approach her. She was so above him. Above all of us. And seeing her, once for his part, and twice for mine, should have been enough to last a lifetime, without seeking hopelessly for more.

I was just trying to resign myself to that very thought, when to my surprise and delight, I caught sight of her again. She had appeared from a door below the stage, sliding unobtrusively into the aisle of the theatre, while the spectators were all distracted by the show on the stage. I saw her slip through the crowd, the diaphanous strips of red silk once more seeming to flow from her body, and pass onto the stairs and ascend, her superb body seeming to glide rather than walk, with all the grace of a dancer.

For a wild moment, I thought she was coming to see me, but then I dismissed the thought from my mind. Instead, therefore of looking to the door of our box, I leaned forward to peer across into the grand box opposite. There, lit by the faint orange glow of the artificial candles in their sconces, a moment later she appeared. In the dim light, her black hair seemed to shine, as did her silks and her perfect flawless skin.

The three inhabitants of that box rose to their feet as she entered and bowed low to her, smiling and saying something I could not hear. Yet, with a graceful movement of her hand, she ushered them back into their seats and came to stand in front of them. Then, with slow, sensual movements, she began to undo the silks and allowed them to slip from her body, appearing to caress it as they fell, and she stood naked in front of the three figures, swaying gently with the music. She reached her arms above her head and even more slowly still performed a perfect pirouette. As she turned, I saw once more her perfect breasts, so full and rounded and dark with their beautiful dark nipples that I yearned to kiss, to suck on, and I saw too the curve of her firm, smooth stomach, and the slender line of her pubic hair, and those thick, luscious thighs. I felt myself grow hot merely looking at her, but I felt something more too, a kind of desperation, a longing to be close to her, to touch her, to caress her, that was so powerful I thought my chest, my mind, my whole body would tear itself apart with the sheer strength of the desire. Whatever those three in the grand box had paid for this private display, I felt I would give double, treble, quadruple it, that I would happily ruin myself to be in their place. If only I were rich, I thought. Yet I had not even had the money to pay the entrance fee. My friend had paid it for me. I stared at her transfixed as she completed her turn, gazing at the cascading waves of her hair flowing down the smooth, tanned back, and at the perfectly shaped contours of her arse, and at her long legs, and all of the noise of the show on the stage below, all of the people and lights and music seemed to disappear, leaving me staring in silence, alone but for those four figures across from me. Then I realised, in a sudden moment of clarity that seemed to fill my heart with a fire of the most intense jealousy I had ever experienced in my life, that the unveiling of her body was not the only pleasure to which the three in the box were to be indulged. With the same grace as her every other moment, my dark princess had dropped to her knees in front of the woman, who with a cry of delight lifted her dress and spread her legs wide to receive her. Those full, faintly upturned lips, kissed languidly, sensually up the bare thighs of the woman, and then lips and tongue made contact with the woman's sex and remained there. The woman watched her for a minute or two, running her fingers gently through the gleaming black hair, and then all of a sudden it was as though a bolt of electricity had shot through her and she flung her head back, gripping the dark princess's own head tightly between her thighs, her eyes wide and wild, and from her lips, over even the tumult of the crowd, came faintly a cry of ecstasy that went on and on as her body shook beneath her, until she had thrust the woman who gave her so much pleasure from her, almost violently, and had collapsed, trembling and gasping, a look of blissful, almost insane satisfaction on her face.

  The dark princess moved on hands and knees, with her head raised and back arched so that her arse stood up beautifully, tantalising as her movements, from between the legs of the woman to place herself between those of the man beside her. Looking at him in the eye, her slender hands reached out to slowly unbutton his trousers and to withdraw from them what lay within. Then her head bowed once more and she began to pleasure him with her mouth with the same exquisite expertise as she had the woman. Like that woman, the man began by simply gazing down at her, a smile of pride and satisfaction on his face, yet, as with the woman, within what seemed an almost impossibly short period of time, his head too was thrown back and I could see his hips thrusting wildly upward as he attempted to present himself as fully as possibly to the delights of those perfect lips and tongue. And then his hands had gripped the arms of his chair so hard that the knuckles showed white and the muscles of his shoulders and upper arms seemed to strain against the fabric of his dinner jacket and almost a bellow of ecstasy escaped him. The dark head in his lap went on moving slowly up and down, and I could picture her face, beautiful and tranquil while she sucked gently, languorously, prolonging the last waves of his orgasm to the point at which he must almost have gone mad at the pleasure of it. Leaving him at last, she made her way on hands and knees, her hips swaying, her head once again held high and proud, to the last man and repeated the performance one last time. When she had reduced him likewise to a state of quivering, mindless silence, she rose finally and dressed with such beautiful, sensual movements that to watch her to do so was almost more erotic even than it had been to watch her strip down to her previous state of nakedness. The men and the woman, each reached out to clasp her hands, mouthing words of immense gratitude, and pressing money upon her and even the jewelled necklace and bracelet the woman had worn. And then she had turned from them and seemed to glide from the box back to the staircase and then down through the crowd, who watched her hungrily as she passed, to the stage door and through it and out of sight.

When she was gone, I felt that curious emptiness that comes after making love – when all emotion is stilled, all desire sated, all thoughts banished from mind. Though I had not touched her, though I had watched only from afar as she gave pleasure to others, it felt as though I had myself made love to her, caressed her and arrived at the state of ecstasy in her arms. It was one of the most erotic moments of my life.

That night when I returned home and lay in bed, I could not sleep for the image of her in my mind. She haunted me, naked and beautiful and wanton, yet still with that air of untouchability, of gentle, quiet detachment from the world. I pleasured myself while picturing her doing for me what she had done for the woman in the box, hoping that by doing so I would be able to forget her a moment and rest. But when I came, convulsed by an orgasm so powerful that it left me shaking and drained, the image departed for a few moments only before it returned and caused me to grow hot and wet again and desperate with the want of her.

The next day, sitting in the café, I found her there once more, where I had all but giving up the idea of seeing her again. I looked across at her eagerly, expecting to see the face that had haunted me throughout the night, but in place of the sensuous, sultry temptress of the previous evening, I saw only the beautiful, untouchable, peaceful woman, with her coffee before her and her wonderful dark eyes smiling gently down as they ran across the words in the book in her hand; too perfect to be approached, too flawless to evoke any desire but the desire to worship her from afar.

I never did speak to her. I borrowed money and went to watch her four nights in a row, seeing her performance on the stage, and then her performance in the grand box and almost eating my heart out in jealousy, and each night coming home and pleasuring myself furiously at the image of her, not as she was in the daylight, but as she was in the theatre. Then I gave up going and stopped visiting the café too. She was too lovely, too hypnotising, too unreal. The image of her was like the source of some dark addiction that I knew I might throw my whole life away in pursuit of and get no nearer to. If I had not stopped going to her show and looking for her in the streets then, I imagined that I would never have been able to do so. Yet, oh yet, I am still haunted by her; I still think of her. And I suspect I always will. While the world contains such marvels, it seems to me that it must easily compete with any religious concept of paradise I have ever heard, and the thought of crossing paths with another such marvel is what gives me a thrill each time I step out of my door and into the world.

# ACROSS A NARROW STREET

When I first returned to Granada from Paris, I rented a room on the third floor of a house a street away from the school where I was to study Spanish. The house stood on one of the narrow, cobbled streets at the bottom of the hill of what had once been the Arabic quarter of the city. The hill had once been the Arabic quarter, and there its foot at least the Arabian world lived on. The streets were full of shisha bars and tiny bazaars selling leather goods and lamps and rugs and silver tea sets and tiny fountains which filled the nights with the sound of a gentle tinkling. The air was always heavy with the scents of incense and oils and on Fridays you heard the haunting sound of the adhan ringing out between the buildings. There was a strange intimacy about those streets, which unnerved me to begin with. They were so narrow that you felt almost as though, were you to reach out of your window, you might tap upon the glass of the windows of the house opposite. For the first few days, I found that lack of distance unsettling. Several times, I forgot to close my shutters when I dressed having come out of the shower and it was only when I was fully clothed once more that I realised that my naked body would have been clearly visible to anyone looking out from the flats opposite. The idea of strangers looking at me did not embarrass me any longer. Quite the opposite. However, the idea that someone might think that I was purposefully displaying myself to them, or to their partner, and resent me because of it, made me blush. It was one thing with strangers whom one might never see again, but quite another with neighbours whose liking or resentment might make or destroy one's enjoyment of living somewhere. And it was not only in dressing that I found myself so keenly aware of the proximity of others. That first week, when I came home with one of the other students of the school and we made love, I stifled my cries of pleasure for fear that they would carry across to the bedrooms in which those neighbours lay.

As time passed, however, I became less self-conscious; less fearful of the eyes and ears that surrounded me. In part this came from familiarity. With all sensations and experiences, time and repetition remove all but the deepest discomfort or fear. For another part, however, I worried less simply because I had come to realise that compared to one set of neighbours in particular, those on the other side of the street, my life and actions could provide no very exciting spectacle.

These neighbours I speak of were a couple who lived in the flat directly across from my room, whose shutters I never once saw closed in all the time I lived there. The desire to keep anything hidden from the world around them seemed a desire that was apparently completely alien to them. For them, to walk naked from the bathroom to their bedroom to dress, or into the living room to lie down on the sofa to drink a cup of coffee or a glass of something whilst all the while dressed in nothing at all, seemed to evoke neither shame nor fear. Equally, to make love with the shutters open and the lights on so that they might be heard and seen by anyone on the other side of the street was to them, it appeared, the most natural of actions; actions that no-one could be troubled by. Indeed, I wonder how many people were ever troubled by it. They were both so beautiful to watch; the man tall and lean, with an athletic body every part of which seemed to have been modelled on along the lines of a Greek statue. Every part that was except his cock which would have put any Greek statue to shame. The woman meanwhile looked like a doll – but a sensual, eminently desirable doll. She was less than medium height, perhaps five feet one or two and had very glossy black hair that seemed always to hang over one eye. Her waist was narrow, her breasts very round and firm, her arse round and firm too and her legs shapely and milky smooth. The features of her face all appeared exaggerated. Her eyes were huge and dark, made to appear even larger by the heavy dark eyeshadow she wore. Her lips were thick and pillowy and upturned and perpetually half-parted; lips that begged to be kissed. Her skin was exaggeratedly flawless and her dark lashes absurdly long, and her ears made to seem smaller and more delicate by the huge hoop earrings she always wore. From the first moment I saw her, I remember thinking that there was something deeply sexual about her. Perhaps it was those lips, so inviting, or those dark, sultry eyes, or simply the obvious fact that she was so frequently naked. Or, and for myself I think this last most likely, perhaps it was that she had garters tattooed about her pale thighs, and more tattoos that resembled manacles on both her wrists and ankles.

When the couple made love, *she* made no effort to stifle her cries of pleasure. In fact she made enough noise that people two streets away must have been aware of what she was doing. Sometimes she was so loud that I wondered fleetingly if she were merely putting on a show. Yet, despite the volume of her cries, there was such a quality of naturalness about their tone that I was forced to admit to myself that they were in fact completely genuine; that her lover simply brought her that quantity of pleasure – her lover, or her usage of him.

Sometimes, taking care to stand where I thought I was least likely to be seen, I would watch them and marvel. I marvelled at the power and confidence each seemed to display; at the way they took from each other exactly what they desired, and gave with equal ardour. Their bodies seemed always to move in harmony, one with the other. There was never any awkwardness to their movements; never any uncertainty. They appeared to understand, without the need of speech, exactly what the other wanted and would do next, and so their movements flowed like a beautifully erotic piece of choreography. And yet this never seemed the result of a form of mundane repetition as with many couples. Every time I watched them, their love scenes played out differently, never losing that air of excitement and newness. Had they wanted to devote themselves to making pornography, they might have made a fortune. Yet apparently they had no desire to do so, since I never saw a camera present. They made love for the reason all people should make love; for pleasure, for joy, for ecstasy, for themselves, and one another. I wanted desperately, hopelessly to join them in their love-making. Yet, to me, this always seemed a vain desire. They seemed so happy in one another's arms, so perfectly matched to one another, that I felt sure they never even thought of involving anyone else in their bliss. I was to find, however, that in that thought at least I was mistaken.

One night, I remember, I had come home early with a young man I had met in a bar that afternoon. We had drunk a last glass of wine together in bed, and then made love and the two things, combined with the warmth of the night, had sent him to sleep almost immediately after our orgasms had faded. For my own part, however, I did not feel like sleep at all, and quietly got out of bed and poured myself another glass of wine and took it to the windowsill to look out and breathe in the scents of the Spanish night.

Across the narrow street, the shutters of the flat opposite were, as ever, flung wide open and the lights of the bedroom and the living room leading off from it burned brightly, illuminating every inch of space in perfect detail, from the unmade bed to the black and white photographs of flamenco dancers and galloping horses upon the walls. And there, in the middle of the living room was the couple I had so often caught glimpses of before, apparently unconcerned by the spectacle they were providing to any who might glance in their direction. The man was fully dressed in dark jeans and a fitted black tee-shirt, but the woman, that beautiful, almost unreal woman with her silky black hair and flashing eyes and the tattoos on her thighs and ankles and wrists, was naked but for a pair of pale blue stilettos. They were kissing passionately, the woman pressing her body against the man's, running her fingers through his hair while the man's own hands caressed her from waist to neck. I remember thinking that there seemed to be something of desperation in those kisses. They appeared as the last kisses shared by a couple that knows that one must slip away before the dawn and may never be able to return; as though each were intent on consuming the other, in drawing from them every last atom of passion before it was too late. Unconsciously, I sat down on the windowsill to watch them, forgetting that I might be seen by them, or that my own lover might awake and want to know what I was doing. They were too captivating, they created too wonderful an image, for either of those thoughts to cross my mind. Quite the contrary, it seemed to me the most natural thing in the world to watch them, as one watches the sunset over the sea or a full moon rise above a range of snow-capped mountains.

After a few minutes of watching, however, to my disappointment, from the depths of the flat, the doorbell sounded and the man suddenly stopped his impassioned kissing of the woman and held her from him. I glanced down from my window and saw that in the street below there was a small group of men waiting on the doorstep of the entranceway to the couple's building. Upstairs, across from my room, the man did not immediately go to answer the door, but instead turned from the woman and went into the bedroom where he took what looked like several long, wide strips of black silk from the drawer by the side of the bed. Returning to the living room, he kissed the woman once more – a long, lingering, passionate kiss – then whispered something in her ear and turned her away from him. He took one of the strips of silk and I watched as he used it to blindfold her, wrapping it across her eyes before tying it firmly in place at the back of her head just below the high ponytail she wore that night. He took a second strip of silk and used it to bind her hands behind her back, covering the tattoos on her wrists. Finally, with the last strip of silk, he bound her ankles together, and then, placing a hand upon her shoulder, he gently pushed her down to her knees in the middle of the room before turning from her and walking away toward to door of the flat that led out onto the staircase. My gaze did not follow him, but remained with her, kneeling as she was, bound and blindfolded on the Moorish carpet. I do not think I have ever seen a more erotic sight in all my life. Nor could I ever have imagined one. In my imagination, the eroticism of the moment would have been tempered by its unreality. Yet here, brightly lit before my eyes, the truth and reality of the image was pure and intoxicating. And the arousal I felt in looking at it, was only heightened by not knowing what would come next. Would he leave her behind like that, to await him for hours while he went out to laugh and drink with the men downstairs? Or would he merely speak with them briefly, before returning to ravish her, helpless to resist as she was having placed herself, her body, completely in his hands, to use and enjoy as he desired. I wished I knew how it felt to be her in that moment; to kneel there in total darkness, feeling the smooth silken bonds holding me rigidly, vulnerably in place and the soft rug beneath my knees, listening for the sounds of my lover's return, uncertain what he had planned for me, what form his pleasures might take, yet ready to submit to them, whatever they might be, and to receive pleasures in return.

Behind her, I saw the door of the flat open once more and saw too that I had been mistaken in both of my predictions. The man did re-enter the room and came to stand before the woman. Yet he was not alone. Behind him, the group of men from the doorstep had entered also and came to stand beside him, forming a circle around the beautiful, bound woman kneeling naked and vulnerable on the floor. I gasped as I realised what was going to happen next. The man, my neighbour, was going to give her to them, to let them take their pleasure with her, as he had taken his own pleasure so many times before. There were four of them. Two were young, in their early twenties perhaps, with short cropped black hair and athletic figures clearly discernible beneath their tailored white shirts. The other two were older than I had thought when I had glanced down at them in the street; in their early to mid-forties perhaps; one immensely tall and broad, with blond hair shaved almost to nothing and faint shadow of stubble on his cheeks, dressed in an immaculately cut suit; the other, of medium height, wearing a black vest that fitted him like a glove and revealed heavily muscled arms and shoulders, covered in an intricate web of tattoos.

At a word from my neighbour, those four strangers all moved in closer, almost but not quite blocking the woman before them from my view. The younger two merely gazed down her, examining that lovely body in minute detail, from the lush, plump thighs and shaven sex, to the firm round breasts with their pouting, brown nipples. The two older men, however, reached down boldly to touch her; one gently running his fingers across those breasts, before cupping them in his hands, feeling the weight of them, and then lightly twisting the nipples between large, tanned fingers; the other, his knees bent to bring him closer to her, taking the firm shapely arse in both of his hands, squeezing it and massaging it, before reaching down further with one hand and tracing his fingers over her sex and then slowly up the cleft between her buttocks. He withdrew his hand and spat into it before returning it to its former place to toy excruciatingly languidly with her pussy and exposed anus. I thought I saw a tremble run through her body then, and heard a faint moan of pleasure escape her lips, but perhaps I was merely projecting onto her the sensations that ran through me in watching the scene.

While this went on, the man who had brought them all upstairs, merely stood looking on, with a faintly devilish smile on his lips. I had always imagined that a man who gave his partner to the pleasures of others would look weak; jealous perhaps, or nervous, but certainly pitiful in a way – unmanly. Yet there was nothing pitiful about my neighbour. Neither his self-control, nor the air of rebellion had left him in the slightest. He looked the master of the scene, more attractive and confident than ever. He was enjoying what he saw; enjoying it without shame, or remorse, or envy.

After a minute or two, the man toying with the woman's breasts straightened, took out his cock and pressed it against her lips, which opened at the first touch to let it enter her mouth. She seemed eager, neither nervous nor afraid, nor even surprised. Rocking slowly back and forward on her kneels, her hands still bound awkwardly behind her back, she simply began to fellate him; doing so richly, tantalisingly and with obvious pleasure. And the man let her do so without touching her, only the curve of his lips and the half-closing of his eyes betraying the ecstasy her touch brought him. Meanwhile, around him, the other men one by one took out their own cocks and began to stroke them slowly, their eyes fixed on the woman and on the great, thick member sliding in and out between her lips. Oh, how much I would have loved to be her then. To be the absolute focus of those four handsome men. To feel their presence around me, yet to never to know who any of them were, or what they looked like; to not know whether they were friends of mine, or neighbours; men I had been close to, or had seen every day. And to feel that wonderfully hard cock sliding gently between my lips; to taste it, to feel its smooth tip running across my tongue and pressing against the roof of my mouth, while at the same time I could hear the faint, wet slapping noise as other cocks were masturbated around me; the owners of which were thinking desperately how much they wanted to place themselves in my mouth, or in my pussy which was growing wonderfully hot and wet between my legs.

After a few minutes, the other man who had been bold enough to caress the woman, touched his friend on the shoulder, and the man in her mouth pulled away from her and stepped aside to let him take his place. Again at the first touch of the hard cock against her lips, the woman opened her mouth once more, and again the man left her to pleasure him at her own pace. This second man's cock was shorter than the first, but immensely thick and I could see the woman's lips stretch to fit around it. I thought how full her mouth must feel, how urgently she must have wanted to have it in her pussy instead, filling her there just as completely, but driving her towards her own climax.

The younger men, when their turns came, were more eager. When they took their places in front of her, they both took her by the ponytail and guided her up and down their engorged shafts, pushing themselves deeper and deeper into her willing mouth, increasing their speed until they were almost fucking her mouth as they would have fucked her sex. Yet if this troubled her in the slightest, it did not show. She submitted without any move to pull away, and I thought even began to rock more quickly, more urgently against their thrusts.

As the second young man grew more vigorous in his enjoyment of her, one of the older men moved closer to her once more and began to rub the tip of his cock against her cheek. The other older man followed suit on the other side. Slipping from the hand that gripped her, the bound young woman began to move between the three of them, slathering each in turn with her tongue, before plunging suddenly forward to take them in her mouth, her rhythm increasing all the time while the men thrust themselves forward, competing for her blind attention.

I thought the scene must come to end within moments then; that soon one or other of the men would be able to stand the pleasure she gave them no longer, and that they would fill her mouth or cover her cheeks and exposed breasts with their come, and that the image of which would set off a chain reaction amongst the others. Yet this was not the case. Finally, one of the older men, the largest of them, the great tall man with broad shoulders and thick, strong arms, lifted her gently to her feet yet at the same time keeping her bent double so that youngest man's cock remained in her mouth. Then he knelt down behind her and buried his face between the cheeks of her arse, his tongue reaching out to lick and massage her sex. This time I knew that the shudder of pleasure I saw run through her and the moan that escaped her lips were not imaginary. The shudder was too visible; the moan, though muffled by the beautiful smooth cock in her mouth, too clearly audible across the narrow alleyway. She thrust her arse back eagerly, grinding herself against his tongue, but before she could climax, he stood up and taking his large cock in his hand, began to rub it back and forth over her dripping sex. I saw her move to press back against it, just as I would have done in her place, yet for a time he kept it from her, allowing only the tip to slide back and forth between her pussy lips. What torment she must have been suffering, I thought as I watched her. I knew that feeling; to be brought to the height of pleasure by lips and tongue, to be driven almost wild by desire, and then to have one's lover withhold the one thing for which one's body cried out so desperately. The woman, seemed to indeed be suffering just as I imagined her to be for she raised her head to say something, the cock on which she had been sucking slipping momently from her mouth. Before she could get out a word of supplication, of command, however, a hand had taken her by the ponytail and pushed her head back down toward another cock that waited, impossibly hard and almost visibly throbbing, for her to bring it pleasure.

Though I hardly expected him to be, the man behind her was merciful. He ceased his teasing almost immediately and, taking a gently hold of her by one hip, he guided that massive cock back to the entrance of her sex and eased it inch by inch inside her. This time, the moan she let out was so loud that the vibrations of it running through the cock in her mouth caused the man being sucked by her to let out his own moan of pleasure and thrust forward wildly. As if in response, the man behind her, began to make love to her with long, slow, strokes, drawing back to the point where only the tip of his great cock remained inside her, before driving himself deep, deep, deep into her pussy. Her stifled moans grew in frequency and intensity. Her back arched, allowing him to move further inside her. Her limbs seemed to tremble and her mouth fell open, allowing the man before her to guide himself in and out over her tongue at his own pace. And all the while, the other two men stood one on either side of her, running their cocks across her cheeks, or else reaching down to caress and tease her breasts.

At last, the man who had been fucking her, grasped her lightly around the waist, lifted her away from the men at her mouth and carried her to the sofa where he lay her down, undid the restraints that bound her legs, and eased them apart. For a minute or two, the other men watched as he bathed her sex in the attentions of his tongue, then once more he entered her, drawing from her a cry of pleasure that rang through the room and out into the street. Another man bent to kiss and suck her upthrust breasts, followed quickly by another. Then the final man came to stand by her head and once more pressed his cock to her lips.

After a few minutes, the first man to have entered her was pushed aside and another man took his place, followed by another, and another. And on it went. One by one they took turns in making love to her, hardly giving her a moment's pause between them, while at the same time, those not between her legs, worshipped her breasts or fought for a place in her mouth. For her own part she seemed almost possessed. Her body moved wildly, sensuously, grinding itself against the cock in her sex, against the sofa, against the lips at her breasts, writhing in serpentine movements of pure ecstasy. At one point, after the bonds that held her arms behind her back had been stripped off, she pushed all of the men away and took hold of a single cock and guided its owner onto his back and mounted him, whilst with her other hand she grasped the nearest cock within reach and began to stroke it frantically. Her head went back and her cries of pleasure rang out, sounding startlingly loud across the narrow street. All while her lover looked on from the seat he had taken, with a libertine expression of satisfaction on his face.

She came on one man, and then a second, all the while sucking and masturbating the others, grabbing her breasts, and playing with herself in a kind of wild, ecstatic frenzy. When the second orgasm had faded, the man below her, who had had his face buried in her breasts as she rode him, lay back and pulled her towards her, easing her further down onto his cock and keeping pulling her body down until her breasts were pressed against his chest and her arse was raised, exposed to the men who stood looking down at her. For a moment they stood still, watching as she drove herself shakily up and down the cock in her pussy, moaning and calling out each time it filled her. Then one of the younger men bent down and lapped at her exposed anus with his tongue, ignoring the balls of the man she rode which we slapping wildly against her. He licked across her anus and around it and then inserted the tip of his tongue the tiniest of fractions. She seemed to freeze in motion as she felt him there and I wondered for a split second if she were going to try to pull away. But she did not. She merely reached back and took hold of him by the back of the head and forced his face deeper between her buttocks, urging him to lick her more deeply, gasping and moaning as she did so. Her writhing seemed to increase with the new sensation, until finally with one final, wild shriek of joy, she came for a third and final time and collapsed forward onto the man in below her.

For a few moments, they let her rest. Then she was lifted gently from the sofa and placed on her knees in the centre of the room and once more the men formed a circle around her each stroking their hard cocks with increasing urgency.

At a command from her lover, she tilted her head back, thrust her breasts forward and opened her mouth. I found myself biting my lip with anticipation for how I knew then the scene would end. Then it did, as one by one they took it in turns to step forward and shoot their sperm all over her. I saw jets of come shoot into her open mouth and spurt across her cheeks and forehead. It ran across the silken blindfold and down her chin and over her upthrust breasts, sliding down, down over her body onto her thighs. And as each man finished, he moved closer to her and thrust his dripping cock into her mouth and watched as she sucked it gently, swallowing the last drops that flowed from it. I felt then, almost as though I could taste the men's sperm, feel it on my own cheeks and across my body, silken smooth and warm. My neighbour himself stepped up to her last. Taking out his cock, which was almost impossibly hard and already seeming to tremble with the pleasure that ran through it, he thrust it into her mouth and watched with an expression of wildest pleasure on his face as she sucked it, quickly, urgently for a few moments, and then he too had pulled out and added his come to that already spattered across her cheeks and breasts.

And then it was all over. Then men, shakily dressed themselves and having spoken to the man of the couple, they shook hands with him and left, glancing back only as they went out of the door, at the beautiful woman, kneeling still on the carpet, her face and body covered in their sperm. Only once they had left, did my neighbour go back to the woman, ease her to her feet and remove the blindfold. She blinked up at him, her eyes wide and glazed by pleasure, and then she smiled and the man shook his head wonderingly and smiled back. She disappeared, walking uncertainly, shakily, into the bathroom where she remained for some time. When she reappeared, she was looking flushed and clean, and she kissed the man as passionately as she had before his guests had arrived, then fell onto the bed and was asleep a moment later with a look of contented bliss on her face. What I would have given to be her, I thought then, as I slipped from the windowsill and back into my own bed beside my sleeping lover. What I would have given to experience the same thing she did. Yet for me, the lover, self-confident enough, enough untouched by jealousy, to facilitate and enjoy such an experience with me, and to go on loving me, wanting me, delighting in me afterwards, has yet to appear.

# THE GENTLEMAN

### PART ONE

He had been coming to the bar almost every night for two weeks; a tall man, always immaculately dressed, of an age that was hard to discern. His face was handsome and youthful, but his dark hair and stubble were faintly flecked with grey. He gave off an aura of money. Not new money; brash and visible. But the type of money that makes one confident in everything one does, without feeling the need to brag or make display. He had beautiful manners and never seemed to count the cost of anything. Yet his clothes, though well fitting and stylish, all black or white, were neither pretentious nor bawdy, nor designed to call attention to themselves. He spoke to me in English, but whenever anyone else spoke to him he proved that his Spanish was flawless, and even faintly flecked with the accent of the city. I think, that like us, he was some sort of writer, but one who wrote for pleasure rather than for money, since when I asked him what he wrote he told me only that he was working on a few novels that he doubted anyone would ever publish, and he said it as though he could not have cared less if they did or not, though this might have been a sham. Why he came to the bar each night, I was not sure, but I liked having him there. He would sit at the bar, with a notebook in front of him, writing with concentration for a time before pausing to speak to me for a few minutes. He was charming and funny, and when he looked at me, I felt a spark of something between us. A part of me wanted to believe that he came there for me, to see me, to speak to me, but he made no tangible sign of it. He never asked if I had a boyfriend, nor invited me to go for a drink with him, nor asked any private questions, nor made any overt compliments such as men who are interested in women usually make. Not knowing what he wanted, disconcerted me a little. Yet another part of me was glad of it. It meant that there was never any awkwardness between us. He was a charming customer and I was the barmaid to whom he liked to talk, to make laugh, to watch pouring his drinks. Nothing more. That was what I thought at least for those first few weeks, but of course I was mistaken. Perhaps you will have noticed from my narrative thus far, the common thread of my life has been my mistaken perception of people and myself.

One night we were talking of nothing, when a lottery vendor came in and I bought a ticket. There had been some sign that afternoon, I forget what, that had made me think I was going to be very lucky in the near future, and so I bought the ticket because I have never been a person capable of letting such signs pass them by without acting on them. He laughed at my eagerness and when I had put the ticket carefully in my purse and come back to him, he asked why I was so excited.

"Because I know I am going to win," I told him.

He smiled; not a patronising smile but one that seemed simply of pleasure at my enthusiasm.

"And what would you do, if you won the lottery?" he asked.

I shrugged.

"When I win," I corrected. "What would anyone do? I will travel. I want to go to Cuba and to Colombia and Argentina. I want to see the Andes and eat big meals and drink Mojitos in some rundown bar on the beach while music plays and all the local people dance tango."

He waved a hand dismissively.

"But a person does not need to win the lottery to make that trip. With ten thousand euros, a person could see all of those places and have a fine time doing so."

I laughed at him then and shook my head.

"And who do you suppose would give me ten thousand euros?" I wanted to know. "Or do you think that were I to put my tips into a jar, I could save it myself in a few months?"

"I might give it to you," he said. His voice still contained amusement, yet there was a hint then of something else in it too, a hint of sincerity perhaps, that knocked me off my stride.

"Of course," I replied, trying to make my voice one of light-hearted mockery, as though I had not heard his change of tone. "I am sure that from the goodness of your heart you give all the barmaids ten thousand euros."

He smiled again, a gentle smile this time, but one in which a certain devilishness, certain unspoken desires, seemed present.

"No," he said, the sincerity in his voice seeming suddenly to become more dominant than the amusement. "Not from that. But in return from something from you, I might."

I had been drying a glass while we spoke, but at those words I put it on the bar and looked at him intently, searching unconsciously for something in his eyes, some sign of whether he were making a joke or not. It was impossible to say. There was no lewdness in his statement. No suggestiveness. By all measures it was merely a statement of fact. Yet, I assumed I must have misunderstood it or misheard it, or that he had simply mistaken his tone, since it did not seem possible to me that a man who appeared to be in every respect the gentleman could have honestly meant to imply a proposition. I decided to act as though he *were* making a joke and adopted a tone of sceptical amusement, as such a joke between friends would call for; though it dawned on a part of me in that moment that we were not friends at all, but little more than strangers.

"Oh, yes. I am sure," I said. "In return for what? For a smile? Or were you thinking of a kidney?"

He looked at me penetratingly for a moment, and then the corner of his mouth ticked up in a smile that resembled nothing so much as when a man lays his cards upon the table knowing even before seeing the hands of his opponents that he has won.

"One night," he said, lowering his voice so that no-one nearby would hear his words. He said it calmly, his blue eyes not leaving mine, and there was no longer any question of whether he were joking. "Were you to give yourself to me," he went on, "truly give yourself to me from sunset to sunrise, willingly and completely, that might be worth your ten thousand euros."

A hundred thoughts at once began to run through my mind then, I remember. I wondered how he could have the audacity to suggest that to me. I wondered if I should tell him that he disgusted me, or swear at him, or simply turn coldly away and refuse to serve him again. He had, I told myself, just offered me ten thousand euros to serve as his whore for a night. Did he do that with every barmaid he met? Or was it simply me? Was there an aura I was giving off of being available to the highest bidder? Of having no more moral character than to sell my body to *any* stranger who offered for it? And yet… and yet he was not any stranger. He was handsome and amusing and he was unafraid of me. And perhaps I did have no more moral character than his offer implied. Was I not the same woman who had watched the two prostitutes please my neighbour with such envy and desire? I should have sworn at him or sent him away or been cold toward him, but I did none of those things. I heard myself say only; "You could have an escort for a tenth of that, you know."

"Of course, I could," he replied with a shrug, his smile not leaving his full lips. "But then again, so might anyone else. And I do not like to think of myself as *anyone else*. From life, I desire those things that are not available to just anybody; those things, and sensations, and experiences that are rare and beautiful; that are truly worthy of remembering."

I stared at him a moment longer. What was it about him that made his words sound so reasonable, even tempting? Was it simply that he was unafraid, unashamed of uttering them? Or was there something else?

"Are you so rich that you can throw around ten thousand euros for a single night?" I asked.

"Rich enough," he said. It did not come across as vulgar boast. It was said as a mere admission of the true state of affairs.

"And what if I said that ten was not enough and asked for fifty?"

"In that case I might take my ten thousand and leave."

"Or you might give it to me."

He shrugged again.

"That would be a gamble on your part."

He glanced at an expensive watch I had not previously noticed on his wrist and, placing the money for his drinks on the bar with his usual tip, he stood up.

"I do not believe in pressurising people," he said. "My offer is real and I will leave you to consider it. If you decide against it, there is no need for you to say anything. We will simply never mention it again. But if you decide that it interests you, well, simply let me know and we will make an arrangement."

And like that, he smiled at me again, that bright and charming smile, and then turned and walked out of the bar into the street beyond.

    I watched him go feeling conflicted, and remained conflicted all that night as I worked, functioning on autopilot, hardly noticing what I was doing or who I was talking to. My mind was a whir of thoughts and emotions and desires. I wanted to feel insulted. Yet I had to admit to myself that I was not. He had been too charming, too polite, too much the gentleman. He had made me an offer, and made it equally clear that I was under no obligation either to accept it or to speak of it again if I did not care to. Yet what an offer it was. To be valued at ten thousand euros was a form of compliment, I supposed. If one were to sell one's body to a man, it was not an insulting price. It was nearly a year's wages for me at that moment. A year's wages, for one night. For a night that I might even enjoy. Was it really such a terrible thing? Such an outrageous suggestion? I imagined myself with him; making love with him. I imagined him taking me in his arms and kissing every inch of me. I imagined his fingers stroking me, teasing me, and then him entering me, his body gliding lightly over mine, while his hard sex drove deeper and deeper… Yet, I told myself, that was unlikely to be the kind of sex a man who was willing to pay ten thousand euros would want. He would want me to pleasure him, to put me on my knees and have him suck his cock. To humiliate me. To fuck me in the arse. To come all over my face. To whip me, perhaps. To chain me to the bedpost. Yet, as I imagined all of those things, I found my mind more aroused still. I wanted those things from him. I wanted that fantasy of a man owning me, taking his pleasure from me, caring nothing for me, and yet paying me to be his and bringing me pleasure in spite of his inclinations. I would receive pleasure, I began to know that. And it would be exciting, dangerous even. More even than the money itself, I thought, and those thoughts gave me pause. But the money too played its part. To be able to travel, to see the world, to live, without thinking of money for a time, was an experience I had almost forgotten. Ten thousand euros for one night; for one night with him. When I arrived home that night, I told the girl I was living with about his offer and, having asked me for a description of him, her advice was simple.

"Do it," she told me.

"You do it," I shot back instinctively.

"I would," she said, with all sincerity, "but he did not make me the offer. If you can get him to offer for me instead, I will. What is there to lose? If he is a gentleman, he will treat you well. And if he doesn't treat you well, run. But run with his ten thousand euros in your purse."

I am not sure if that was what decided me to do it, or if were the dreams I had that night. I dreamed I was giving myself to him, and that he was taking me, and I dreamed of how powerful I felt and of how aroused and of how even the humiliation he tried to subject me to empowered me further and aroused me more deeply. And when I awoke, I was wet and excited and I pleasured myself thinking about serving his darkest desires and orgasmed within moments of touching myself. Perhaps it was that that decided me, or my friend's words, or ten thousand euros for which I would not have to work eight hours a day through a whole year to earn and at the end of the year find it had already gone. I have never been able to decide which.

In the bar that night, I told him that I would accept his offer and he smiled at me and told me that he had thought that I would. That, I found a little jarring; for him to assume my consent to something that no woman should ever, in the eyes of society, consent to. Yet, at the same time, I was aware that he had been quite right in his assumption. There is no justice in punishing someone for their skills of perception. It was, I was sure, his perception that had led him to make me the offer in the first place. Had he thought that I would refuse instantly, that I would be cold with him or insulted, I doubted that he would have asked.

He reminded me gently that in order to receive my ten thousand euros I would need of course to consent to give myself to him completely, to follow his every command, and do so willingly, no matter what he asked, as he had told me when first he made the offer. I agreed, in part. But at the same time I told him there were certain humiliations I would not suffer. When I replied to his question about what form these humiliations might take with a short list, he laughed and told me that no such things would ever have occurred to him. Then I told him that I would want the money the moment I walked in the door, but I agreed, after listening to him, that I would take half on arrival and that the other half he would give me when I left, if I had fulfilled my part of the bargain.

"What is to stop you keeping my five thousand euros at the end of the night?" I asked, having already agreed.
"You could easily cause more damage than that in my flat, if you chose. Besides, what is to stop you taking my five thousand and running?"
"You could stop me," I pointed out. "You are stronger than I am."
He looked vaguely pained by that.
"I hope,"he said, "I am not such a monster. You can leave at any moment you please, I assure you. I will not stop you. But if you want your ten thousand, do not forget that there will be a certain aspect of *earning* it. It is not a gift, I think I said before. I am not so rich as that."
"I will earn it," I told him. "I am accepting your offer in good faith," thinking while the words passed my lips that I might, in that moment, that moment in which I could picture so clearly how it would be to serve him, to pleasure him and be pleasured by him, just as easily have said that I *wanted* to earn it.

When I went the following evening to the address he had given me, I found that it was a flat on the top floor of one of those grand buildings in the Gran Vía that I had looked up at many times and wondered what were the lives of the people who lived there. Now I supposed I was going to find out. The hall through which I passed had marble floors and high ceilings and elaborate mouldings, outlined here and there in gilt. His front door alone, made of polished black wood, had the appearance of being worth more than anything I had ever owned. When I touched the bell beside it, he came to open it almost immediately, greeting me with a smile of welcome and satisfaction. I had done my best to dress in a way that I hoped would please him. I wore a silk top that clung to my body and was cut low to reveal a hint of my breasts, upthrust in a black lace bra. Below, I wore a short black skirt and stockings and finally a pair of black, patent leather, impossibly high heels that I had borrowed from my

room-mate. My hair was loose down my back in curling dark auburn waves, and I had taken care with my make-up, with the deep red shade of my lips and the careful use of mascara and eye shadow; subtle, yet enough to render my eyes smoky and seductive, or so I hoped. The effect did indeed seem to please him. His eyes ran up and down me, appreciatively and he told me, as he closed the door behind me, that I looked beautiful.
"Worth ten thousand euros?" I asked, softly.
"I am sure I will not be disappointed," he replied, and I felt a slight tightening in my stomach as the words left his mouth. I did not want, I realised then, to disappoint him. In all of the fantasies I had ever had of selling myself to a man, the man had always been left all but destroyed by the pleasure I had given him. I did not want in reality to be less than that; to be awkward or unseductive; to fail to identify what would give him pleasure, or to fail to do so in a way that would forever leave him wanting more.

He led me into the living room, a vast room, with three long windows each with its own balcony that looked out across the rooftops of the city. There was a fireplace at one end with an immense sofa and two leather armchairs gathered around it, and a long bar at the other end. Bookshelves covered one wall, and paintings the others, and there were long, heavy velvet curtains at the windows, and thick rugs on the floors. The sound of some sensual classical music played faintly from speakers concealed somewhere amid the furnishings. On a vast sideboard against one wall, lying on a silver tray, there were two envelopes and collar of black leather, such as I had seen slave girls wear in photographs of BDSM fantasy scenes. He went over to these, picked up one of the envelopes first and handed it to me. Inside there was a thick wad of fifty euro notes. Then he gestured to the other.
"That is for you to take when you leave," he said. I nodded and slipped the money into my purse. I could not think of what to say, of what I wanted to say, or what the situation demanded that I should say. He did not seem, however, to

mind my silence. Turning back to the sideboard he picked up the leather collar and held it up for me to see.

"And this, is for you to wear," he said. "May I?"

He approached me and very gently swept my hair to one side and fastened the collar around my neck. It felt cold and rigid against my skin. It was a strange sensation to feel it there. I knew what such collars symbolised – ownership, submission. Men and women wore them when they had agreed to be enslaved, to recognise someone else as having complete power over them. No-one, I thought, had ever had complete power over me. Nor was I sure that I wanted them to. Yet at the same time, that collar seemed to awake something within me; a new kind of desire, a desire to be submissive, to be used, to be the object of pleasure not the one waiting to receive it; the simple act of wearing it seemed to change me, to make me feel subservient, owned, to make the very idea of questioning or refusing any order he might give me, any pleasure he might demand of me, unthinkable.

"Well," he said, stepping away from me. "Shall we begin?"

I nodded but said nothing, and he smiled.

"Good girl," he said, seeming to enjoy my reaction – my silence. "In that case – on your knees."

For a moment I hesitated, wondering whether I should simply run there and then; whether I was truly prepared for what I had agreed to do; whether I wanted to give myself to this man I barely knew, and for him to pay me for doing so, like a common whore. Yet those doubts, I thought, were no more than cowardice. I had thought about it and I had decided that this was what I wanted. If I turned back now, it would be fear that drove me to. And I knew that I would regret it; that I would find myself one day, tired from my work, tired of my life, wondering how it would have been to be paid a vast sum of money, to give myself to this handsome, darkly seductive man of whom I knew so little.

Slowly I knelt, feeling the thick carpet seeming to swallow my knees into it in a warm embrace.

"Good," he said. "Very good. And now I want you to follow me, on hands and knees.
I did so, feeling every inch the slave, the harem girl of my fantasies, and he led me out onto one of the balconies where I found a large armchair and another, smaller rug and a silver table where several tiny lanterns burned.

He settled himself into the armchair and then, there, surrounded by the twinkling lights of the city, where anyone looking out from the top floor windows of the buildings on the other side of the street might have seen me, he had me undress, slowly; to strip off my light silk top, my skirt and then my bra and panties, until I was kneeling before him, dressed only in my heels and stockings and the leather collar around my neck, completely exposed to his hungry gaze.

Then he had me fellate him as I had known he would. No man with a woman completely in his power, willing to do anything that he asked of her, could ever have resisted that. The experience, however, was far more erotic than I would have ever imagined it being. To be there on my knees on a soft rug, naked, while he leaned back in armchair and relished the sensation; to know that any number of eyes might be on me, watching me, wishing they were in his place, wanting me, perhaps even touching themselves, masturbating at the sight of me, filled me with a deep, dangerous pleasure, and a sense of my own power; my own desirability. And he desired me too, more in that moment than he desired any other woman in the world, no matter how beautiful, how untouchable, how perfect, how sultry. With me there, devoting myself to him, elevating him to a new plane of carnal bliss with the caresses of my lips and tongue, the feel of my hot, wet mouth on him, he would have turned all other women aside no matter what inducement they had offered him. I was sure of that, and it excited me.

His soft moans excited me too, as did to the gentle thrust of his hips as he tried, not forcefully or impatiently, but temptingly, yearningly, to ease more of his cock into my mouth. Something about being there on my knees, looking up and seeing the rapture transforming his handsome face, about feeling him throb against my tongue, and hearing him moan, and knowing all the while that it was me that brought him such bliss, that there was nothing he would not having done to keep me there, to keep me pleasuring him thus, that there was nothing in that moment he would have traded it for, made me feel completely womanly, completely aware of my feminine power over him. The collar about my neck excited me, but I was conscious in that moment that it was he who was enslaved to me. That if I had chosen to stop, to leave, he would have been driven almost mad by despair and hunger for me; that he would have begged me to stay, pleaded with me, all of his command and power gone.

And it as not only the general nature of the situation, the experience that I enjoyed. He, himself, the man, was perfect for it. He was so attractive in that moment, so worthy of worship, so gentle and yet so dominated by his desires. His cock is beautiful too. More beautiful than any other I had ever had in front of me. So smooth and flawless, thick and hard in my hand, large, but not so large as to be uncomfortable. It felt wonderful in my mouth. It tasted wonderful too; masculine and yet sweet and clean. It swelled and hardened even more as I sucked it, but its tip was soft and silken against the roof of my mouth, against my tongue. And, when finally I felt him tense, and heard his deep groan of ecstasy and then felt his sweet, hot come filling my mouth, I felt a deep satisfaction all of my own, a luxurious, sensual satisfaction.

He lay back in his chair when it was over, his breath coming out in deep gasps, his eyes filled with amazement and ardour, and I sat back on my knees, looking up at him, tasting him still in my mouth, slowly becoming conscious once more of the city around us, of the lights and open windows and the sound of traffic and voices in the street far below.

"That," he said, when his breathing had slowed and he had gained enough control of his body to put his cock, still half-erect and glistening with the traces of his come that I had left behind, into his trousers and close them once more, "was beyond anything."

I felt myself smile.

"You are welcome," I said. "I am here to serve you."

He rose then to his feet, slightly unsteadily, and lifting me from my knees kissed me passionately for a full minute or two, his hands holding me tight against me. Then, without another word he broke away and lifted me into my arms and carried me through the great living room to an equally majestic bedroom beyond, where he laid me out in the middle of a soft, silk covered bed.

I thought then that he was going to make love to me, that he would take me there, hard and voraciously, and unconsciously I closed my eyes in expectation of the resumption of his kisses. Yet he did not. I felt him move away from me and when I opened my eyes I saw that he was at the dressing table, taking something from the drawers. He came back, a moment later and I saw that what he had retrieved were four wide strips of black ribbon. He smiled at me and motioned for me to raise my hands above my head. I did so, almost nervously. He was going to tie me to the bed, I realised. And once he had done so, there would be no question of who held the power. It would all lie with him. There would be nothing that I could do to resist him, even were I to want to. As he tied my hands to the ornate wooden bedstead, however, I looked into his eyes and saw that though filled still with a lusty hunger, they were kind and trustworthy, and I felt my fear give way.

When my hands were tied, he moved down my body, trailing the ribbons over it so that the cool silk caressed me. Then gently he spread my legs wide and tied one ankle to each bedpost, spread-eagling me, leaving me open and vulnerable to whatever whim crossed his mind. The desire that filled him, however, was not that which had I had expected. Stripping off his shirt, he knelt over me, and began by kissing over my breasts, covering each with the soft, warm caresses of his lips, before sucking gently at my nipples, squeezing them almost imperceptibly between his teeth. I let out a sigh, feeling a warmth building in my own body; a subtle, almost tender desire. And then he was kissing down my stomach, and across my mound to my waiting sex and I felt myself raising my hips, my arms and legs straining a little against their bonds, to press against his mouth. What began with kisses, fleeting, butterfly-like kisses, across every inch of my sex, my inner thighs, my stomach, the exposed part of my buttocks, gave way to a delicious concert of lips and fingers and tongue. With expert touches and caresses, he slowly built my pleasure until at last I was writhing helplessly against my restraints, my whole body alive with trembling, electrifying pleasure that deepened and strengthened, swelling as the waves swell in the midst of a hurricane, before breaking over me in one of the most powerful, most long lasting climaxes of my life to that point.

Afterwards, I hung limp and weak against my bonds, my body so sensitive that even slightest touch of his finger tip seemed to send an unbearable surge of electricity running through me. He left the room then, and when he came back he untied me and pressed a glass of ice cold water into my hand, which I drank like a woman returning from the desert. Then, he pointed to my clothes, which he had brought in and laid out on the bed.

"Time to get dressed now, my beauty," he said and I remember feeling a powerful wave of disappointment sweep over me. Was that all he had wanted of me? Was he now going to send me away? Was there nothing else he had planned for me? It did not, irrationally I know now, seem fair. I had expected a night of pleasure, and had yet to pass more than an hour in his company. I did not say this to him, however, but instead eased myself off the silken sheets, and took my clothes from where they lay. My skirt and top were both there, folded neatly, but when I lifted them I found that my bra and panties were missing.

"I think," I said, sounding almost girlishly innocent my own ears, "that I left my underwear on the balcony."

He laughed, a gentle musical laugh.

"You did," he replied. "I put them with the rest of your money. Later you can take them with you, but for now you will not be needing them."

A fresh thrill ran through me then. So it was not over. There was more to come.

Obediently I pulled on my skirt and top, feeling the silk rub against my still sensitive nipples, and then I turned to face him.

"And now?" I asked.

"Now, we are going out for a drink," he said. Then, seeing my hands move up to my collar, meaning to take it off, he added; "No. I think we will keep the collar on. It will excite me to see you wearing it where all the world can see it too. Just as it will excite me to know that you are beside me, naked beneath your shirt and skirt; available to me at any moment." And so I let my hands drop and allowed him lead me by the hand back through the living room and out into the hall, feeling a new thrill of the unknown that awaited me in the hours of night that remained to us.

## PART TWO

Walking down the street, I saw the eyes of several of the passers-by flicker toward my collar and then to my face. They knew what it meant, I thought, even if the rest of the world seemed unaware. There something intensely erotic about walking down the street, naked but for the thin silk top and short black skirt, feeling the stiff leather collar around my neck; not knowing what was coming next – what he would have me do. Yet wanting to know; hoping that it would be something extraordinary.

He took me to a jazz bar and there we sat on leather topped barstools and drank champagne. Our drinks were served to us by a young man who was dark and handsome and whose eyes kept flickering down to my breasts, whose naked form was clearly visible against the silk. Strangely, this overt objectification did not make me feel angry or dirty. It sent a thrill through me. I had tantalised him with my body alone. He wanted me. He would go home that night and think of me, of the form of my body, and wish that he had had me. Equally he would be jealous of the man beside me; he would imagine all of the things that the man might do to me and would hate him for it. The feeling was one that I liked.

When he had gone off to serve some other people, a waitress appeared in his place and leaned over the bar to kiss the man who had bought me. As she did so, I found myself gazing at her. She was so different from myself. And, I thought then, much, much more attractive. She had that sort of alternative look that works so well on naturally beautiful young women, and so badly on others. She had dark brows and very deep blue eyes, accentuated by a light shadow of make up. Her long hair was dyed a delicate shade of silver purple that gave her beauty a sort of other-worldly quality. Her lips were full and painted a deep red, always slightly parted, poutingly, invitingly, revealing between them stunningly white teeth, the front two of which had a slight gap between them that made her more unusual but detracted nothing from her face. Her skin was pale, and her arms were covered in beautiful drawn tattoos; one of which showed a train of delicate roses rising from her slender wrist, the other a line of humming birds. Her nails were painted black and her hands were small and pale. The rest of her body, even in the loose fitting apron she wore, seemed almost cartoonishly ideal, like that of Jessica Rabbit; her waist slim, her arse rounded and full, and her breasts, or what I could see of them, full too and vaguely pointed. Though she wore white converse where I wore those high, stripper heels, and a simple white shirt, beneath which the straps of a black bra were clearly visible in contrast to my expensive silken top with its lace at the collar and waist, I felt that she put me completely in the shade. I wondered, staring at her, why the gentleman, with her in his life, had chosen me; had paid me and demonstrated his clear desire for me.

The two of them spoke very rapidly in Spanish and very softly, and I, with the music and the sound of voices around me, did not catch what they said. Yet I had the feeling they were talking of me. The girl's eyes kept flickering toward me, to my face, to the collar about my neck, to my chest. And there was, or seemed to be, a knowing gleam in her blue eyes. Who was she? I wondered. Was she like me? Was she another barmaid that he had charmed in the same way he had charmed me? Had she done what I was now doing? Had he bought and kept her for a night to bring him pleasure? The thought inspired me a strange mixture of jealousy and arousal. She was beautiful and would surely be more beautiful without the apron and with her hair loose across her shoulders. Had she pleased him more than I did or would do? Would he really rather have had her again? Or was he happy with me to serve as a contrast? Or had he not had her yet, and was displaying me as a way of tempting her to agree to the same offer he had made me? I made up my mind finally to ask him who she was, but in the end he did not give me the chance. Abruptly the conversation between the two of them stopped and she leaned with her elbows on the bar and surveyed me; almost hungrily, I thought. The man meanwhile leaned close to me and told me in a soft, commanding voice to put my knees up on the bar and spread my legs. I glanced around me. There were many people in the bar, but no-one but the waitress was close to us. The other faces I saw were unfamiliar to me; no friends or colleagues or acquaintances.

"Go on," the man said again. "Do as I tell you."

After one final look around, I did so, but nervously, feeling colour rush into my cheeks as I leant back on my stool and placed my knees on the bar and then slid them open, revealing myself to my gentleman and the waitress. From where she stood, the waitress could see every inch of my naked sex, up close, almost close enough to reach forward and kiss. She looked at it, and smiled, and there a dark glitter in her eyes, just as there had been in the man's. He leaned close to me again and commanded me to play with myself. Why not? I thought. I had agreed to do whatever he wanted. Besides, a part of me wanted to have the waitress see me do so; for her to see my boldness, my sensuality, my wantonness. Slowly, I reached down and began to run the tips of my fingers over myself, feeling myself growing hot and wet as I did so; feeling the tendrils of pleasure rise from my sex through my stomach and thighs, to spread, tingling through my whole body. And while I did so, the waitress's eyes seemed to feast on the sight, twinkling darkly; full of a kind of fiery ardour. The rest of the bar, the people and the music, all seemed to fade into the background and I felt that it was just the three of us there; the man by my side, smiling, the waitress watching so intently, and me. I could feel the first tremors that hinted at an orgasm to come beginning to tingle through my sex.

The man leaned over to the waitress and asked her what she thought; was I what she had in mind?

The waitress kept looking at me with all the intensity of before, and smiled.

"She is perfect," she said.

"Alright," the man said, turning to me then, "you can leave it there."

I stopped touching myself and lowered my legs, but I realised as I did so that I did not really want to. Sitting there, exposing myself, pleasuring myself in front of that beautiful girl while she watched and took pleasure watching, was what I truly wanted. The thrill of it, the danger, the complete lack of shame, all filled me with lust. And while she had looked at me in the way she had, I had felt beautiful too – beautiful and desirable.

We drank the rest of the champagne and by the time we were finished the waitress was beside us, her apron gone, wearing a thin black jacket over her white shirt and with a black clutch under her arm.

"Well," the man said, "shall we go?"

I followed his example and began to get up, but the waitress stopped me.

"Wait," she said. "One more thing."

She opened the clutch and from it she took a slender leash of black leather. She attached the leash to the ring in my collar and then stepped back, running her eyes over me.

"That is better. Now we can go."

Tuning on her heel, she jerked lightly at the leash and began walking to the door, leading me behind her. The man smiled and followed us. If anyone had asked me before that night, how I would have felt to be led through a public bar on a leash like some kind of exotic pet, I am not sure how I would have answered. Yet if I had been honest with myself, I am sure that I would have found the idea darkly thrilling. The experience of it, the eyes of the other clients following me, their sniggers and pointed fingers and remarks, was something I could not have imagined truly until that night. It was humiliating, arousing, freeing. I felt like I was no longer a person but truly nothing more than a willing slave to the will and whims of others. I could feel my cheeks flush again and I could feel my stomach tighten with the fearful realisation that even once the night was over and the collar removed, there would be people all over the city who had seen me wearing it, who had seen me led out on a leash by the waitress with the well-dressed gentleman behind me, walking confidently, projecting the aura of a man who had indeed managed to dominate another person to fulfil his every desires. They would recognise me later, I thought, those people in the bar, and they would remember. And yet, as I walked through the bar after the waitress, feeling the leather about my throat, feeling the eyes of the other drinkers running over my body, I held my head high and my shoulders back and felt proud and desirable at the same moment, and more than that, I felt fearless, knowing that few people could have so publicly shown themselves as I did in that moment.

In the street, the two of them, the waitress and the gentleman, walked arm in arm, while they had me walk in front of them at the end of the leash. And there under the street lamps that first feeling I had had in the bar returned with more strength than that of my pride. I was not a stranger to this part of the city. In fact, where we were walking, we were barely five minutes from where I worked. Anyone might see me. People I worked with, or people who drank regularly in my bar. Or my friends. Or my neighbours. The thought frightened me, but at the same time stirred my arousal almost to fever pitch. I realised that a part of me wanted someone to see me like that. They would be too polite to confront me, to ask me what I was doing, or indeed to mention it to me again in the future, except perhaps in a veiled way. Yet they would carry the image of me being led on the leash down the street, with my breasts almost visible through my shirt, and the collar around my neck, by that handsome couple, home with them that night. They would think, I thought, of all the things that the couple were going to do to me. And they would be stirred. They would wonder what it would be like to take my place, or to take the place of my gentleman; to have a woman with whom they could do whatever they pleased, and who seemed so willing to do it; willing enough to be paraded in public like some slave-girl from a time long past.

Back at the gentleman's flat the waitress kissed me, ran her hands all over my body, and then, with strong, delicate fingers she stripped off my top and skirt. She cupped my breasts, weighing them in her hands, and pinched my nipples until they stood hard, desperate to be kissed, to feel her tongue on them. Then she pushed me firmly down onto my hands and knees and ordered me in a soft, commanding voice, to crawl once around the living room. I did so willingly, feeling again that curious mixture of humiliation and pleasure. I could feel their eyes upon me; the man's from a stool at the bar where he had placed himself; hers from the centre of the room, where she seemed to tower over me, all long legs and large, pointed breasts. When I had completed my circuit, she told me that I was a good girl and stroked my hair as one might caress the head of a faithful dog. Then she told me to take off her own clothes, slowly. I did that too, though my fingers trembled as I undid the buttons of her shirt and slipped it off over her shoulders, and trembled more as I undid her bra and allowed that to fall also. Once her breasts were revealed, however, wonderfully full, high breasts, their light coloured nipples pierced with two silver bars, I forgot my nervousness and felt only desire wash through me. As I reached for the zip of her skirt, I felt suddenly courageous and kissed first one nipple than the other. She let out a tiny purr of pleasure and I felt a tremor run through my sex. Beneath her skirt she wore stockings and French cut knickers of black lace. I moved to take these down too but she caught my hands and held them away.

"With your mouth, puppy," she commanded, the gleam in her eye seeming to become more pronounced and even faintly obscene. So I leaned forward and took the lace between my teeth, drawing the silken underwear over her hips and down her thighs. As my face passed her own beautiful, bare pussy, its lips so soft and puffy, so delicate and yet inviting, I could feel the heat emanating from her, and caught a faint, sweet scent of desire. I wanted to bury my face between her thighs and kiss and lick and worship that pussy; to taste it, to devour it; but she merely stepped out of her knickers and turned from me, giving me a view of her perfectly rounded arse as she crossed the room to the armchair. There she arranged herself with her legs up on either arm, open and inviting. I wanted her so badly then I don't know how I contained myself, but I did not dare follow her. I just stared as she gently stroked her sex, squeezing it and opening so that I could see the little pink clit rising and the deeper pink of her labia. Then, when I felt I could not stay from her any longer, she beckoned me with a finger, as a queen might beckon a servant toward her. Immediately I crawled across to her and placing myself gratefully between her beautifully smooth, ethereally pale thighs, I allowed her to take my head in her hands and ease me down until my mouth was against her sex. My tongue flickered out almost of its own accord and suddenly I was licking her, tasting her honey, relishing the silken softness of her and the heat and wetness. She moaned and held me tighter and I kept licking, sucking at her labia, swirling my tongue across her tiny, engorged clitoris, delving it inside of her, licking, sucking, licking, penetrating. Above me, her moans began to grow louder and I could feel her trembling against me. Then she had moved a little further down in the chair and she pushed my head down too so that my tongue made contact with the tiny knot of anus.

"Lick it," she urged me, commanded me, ordered me. "Go on! Lick!"

I did as she ordered, running my tongue across it and around it, revelling in its smoothness, in the licentiousness of my actions; actions which I had never performed on another person. And she rewarded me with moans and words of encouragement, with blasphemies and gasped exclamations. I wanted to make her come. To taste her. To bring her pleasure, but just before she peaked she took hold of my hair and pulled me roughly away. I looked up at her, knowing that the confusion and disappointment I felt must have been clearly visible to her. Her own face was flushed, her eyes liquid, the gaze glazed by desire and pleasure. I moved to begin licking her again, but she held me away, mercilessly; uncaring of my desperate need to keep going. And then, with legs that trembled slightly she rose from armchair and walked to a cupboard beside where the man sat. The man; I had quite forgotten him. However, as I looked at him now, he smiled at me and I could see this his face too was flushed with pleasure and that in his lap a massive erection was straining at the thin fabric of his trousers. The girl had opened the cupboard and from within she took something out, then she closed the cupboard and kissed the man passionately on the lips. Only when she turned back to me did I see what was in her hand – a long, thick double-ended dildo made of soft black latex. I knew what was coming, and I found I wanted it as desperately as I had wanted to feel her come on my tongue.

With the man watching, she took me by the hand and led me to the sofa where she had me lie on my back and very softly ran the dildo across my cheeks and forehead before bringing it to me lips. It was warm and firm. I sucked it, imagining that it was the man's cock once more, or that it was hers. Or that it was the cock of the dark woman I had watched what seemed like so long ago in the flat of my rich neighbour. Then I felt the man between my legs, kissing passionately up my thighs and then burying his tongue in my sex. The pleasure was immense, rushing through me, throbbing deep within me. I moaned and made to cry out with pleasure, but my moans were stifled by the thick false cock in my mouth. I sucked it almost desperately then, revelling in the twin sensations of my mouth and sex. Then the girl had taken the cock from my mouth and pushed the man away and had me spread my legs wider, as wide as they would go, so that I lay absolutely exposed to both of them in the bright lamplight. The latex cock, which had felt so large in my mouth, felt larger still as she eased it inside of me, thick and long, bigger than any cock that had ever penetrated me. I thought I might burst; from its size, from the pleasure it brought me. I looked down through passion-blurred eyes and saw that the girl was crouching above me, gripping the dildo and easing herself onto the other end. As she pressed it between her lips and into the tight entrance of her pussy, she drove it deeper into me, filling me completely, touching a point of pleasure I had never felt touched before. I moaned and cried out, watching almost hypnotised as she began rising and falling, impaling herself on that thick cock, alternately pulling it from me and driving it deep. I thought I might go mad with the sensation. For a moment I almost blacked out, my eyes shut, my teeth clamping my bottom lip to stifle my cries. And the pleasure kept going on and on, richer with every moment, rising and intensifying. I opened my eyes to look at her, to see if she were experiencing the same bliss that ran through me, and saw the man had come over to kneel beside us. As I watched, he undid his flies and took out his cock. For a moment, I thought he was going to thrust it into my mouth again, and I wanted, I desperately wanted, him to do so. Yet if that had been his intention, before he could do so, the girl had snatched it in her hand and buried it in her own mouth, sucking him, licking him, taking him deep into her throat in a kind of desperate, licentious frenzy. The man groaned and for a moment I thought he was going to come there and then, filling the girl's mouth with his sperm, but before he could do so, the girl had released him and, swinging me with her, she had rolled onto her back so that I was riding her, the dildo thrust even deeper within me, stretching me, filling me. I began to ride her as I would ride a man, in rapture at the pleasure thundering through me and at the look of her, the moans that escaped her as I drove the dildo deeper inside her too. She reached behind me and gripped my arse, then dealt it several stinging slaps on each cheek. The sharp pains, coupled with the waves of the approaching orgasm that raged in my sex, were delicious. I wanted more, but instead I saw her bury two fingers in her mouth, sucking at them, covering them with saliva, and then the fingers were pressed against my anus, fondling it, rubbing it and then finally easing their way inside. The sensation was a fiery one, one in which pleasure and a feeling of violation mingled. And then the man's cock was between us and while the waitress toyed with me, he had me lick it, suck it, and then her hand was in my hair, pushing my head down so that it filled my mouth, until finally he pulled away, leaving behind him the taste of pre-come all over my tongue and lips.

"She's ready," I heard the waitress gasp somewhere beneath me, pulling her fingers out of my arse as she did so. "She's ready. Do it now!"

I felt that beautiful cock, that had just been in my mouth, press against my anus. I felt him drive himself inside of me, filling me, and the joint bliss of the two cocks inside me, thrusting smoothly, rhythmically into me caused me suddenly and uncontrollably to explode in an orgasm that shook my whole body. Below me, the waitress let out a long, amorous cry of her own and began to shake and come too, and then the man was filling my arse with jet after jet of hot sperm that seemed to cause my orgasm to swell to an even greater height.

"Is that what you had in mind?" the man asked the waitress a few minutes later, as I lay on the couch, destroyed, still barely able to summon the energy to lift my head, and they meanwhile sat at the bar drinking a glass of champagne.

"It was better than I had in mind," the waitress replied. "Better than I could have imagined. It is a shame that we cannot do it more often."

"An expensive treat," the man told her. "But there will be others in time."

And lying there, I found myself remembering suddenly what I had forgotten, that they had paid me for what they had just done, that five thousand euros lay in my purse as compensation for the ecstasy they had brought me, and that the man would give me another five thousand as I left, and somehow that made the pleasure greater still. I had sold myself like a highly priced whore, and I had enjoyed it.

# THE ARTIST'S ASSISTANT

How far I had come from those grey, frustrating, unfulfilled days with my first boyfriend. I remember thinking that as I mounted the artist in the garden of his carmen in the bright sunlight where anyone might have seen; as I felt his great, strong, hard cock slide into the wet confines of my sex, filling me, delighting me, sending waves of pleasure running through me; as I saw the look of surprise and ecstasy sweep across his tanned, rugged, time worn face. I had been so restrained with my first boyfriend, so haunted by untasted pleasures, by desires that I did not have the courage to act upon. Yet those days seemed to me then, that warm afternoon, to lie deep in the haze of the distant past. The days of wanting but not taking; of dreaming but not living. The woman I was as I began to ride that perfect cock in state of almost animal frenzy, I realised then, was free of all the insecurities, the doubts, the fears, that had once so completely controlled me. And I was wildly, blissfully happy. I felt him thrust upward to meet my own movements, filling me as deliciously as ever I had been filled, rocking my body with a rapture so powerful that it felt as thought I might pass out from the sheer, wanton pleasure of it, and I gave myself completely to the sensation.

Yet how had I found myself there, that summer's afternoon, beside the glittering pool, feeling the tremors of my orgasm building and building to a peak, while feet from me through the doors of the studio filled its erotic paintings and photographs, two stunningly beautiful models, seemingly oblivious to all that went on outside, were even then laughing and gossiping as they took off their clothes and resumed their poses on the velvet cushioned chaise-lounge on which they had lain throughout the morning?

"If he asks you to do anything that you are not comfortable with, you have only to tell him no, and he will not ask again. He is a sweet old man really, who would do anything for anyone. And he is very generous." That had been what the artist's permanent assistant, Violette, had told me when I had met her to arrange to cover her work for a week while she went on holiday. She had not been explicit about what he might ask me to do, and I did not question her. She seemed happy in her work, and eager to return to it after her break, and she seemed so good and kind that I did not think for a moment that she would put me, a stranger, in a position I would find unpleasant or violating. Yet still, after she had told me what time I was to begin, and how I should start the day, and how the artist liked things to be organised, I went home and spent the night wondering whether I should indeed have asked. The artist was famous, both within the city and throughout the world, for his nude portraits; wonderful, hyperrealistic works, all exotic and beautiful, tantalising and sensual. Might the thing Violette had been hinting at be that he might ask me to pose for him? To take off my clothes in his studio so that he might paint me? If that were what she had been hinting at, I found the thought thrilling rather than uncomfortable. After all, by that time, I had already posed and more before a camera, and found nothing but previously unknown pleasures to be taken from the experience. To pose for a painter, rather than a photographer, would simply be a variation of the same theme; slower in its process perhaps, less explosive in its conclusion, yet a profound, luxuriant thrill nonetheless. If he asked, I decided lying there in my bed, I would not say no.

Yet he did not ask that of me. When I arrived at his house, tucked away behind high walls on the hill opposite the Alhambra palace, I found that there was a list of models already engaged for the week to pose for him waiting on my desk. Also on the desk was a letter of instruction, explaining that my main responsibility was to answer the phone and refer any press requests, or anyone asking any questions at all, to the artist's agent, whose number was written at the bottom of the page. The only exceptions, the instructions said, the only calls that might be put through to the studio, were those of his friends, who would not ask for the artist but instead for "The former lover of Ava Gardner." These, however, would only call in the afternoon since they knew the artist would be annoyed by any interruption before lunch. The models, I should ask to wait, then go through to the studio and check that the artist was ready for them. There seemed to be nothing too onerous in any of that; nothing that I should fear.

When the models arrived, fifteen minutes later than the time written on the paper, they were bright and laughing, careless girls, who seemed to be completely at home in the place. Whatever it was that Violette had been hinting at, these girls, who were accustomed to being in contact with the artist seemed completely happy and confident in entering his house, and I felt that therefore so should I be. And so, while they settled themselves on a sofa, gossiping, I hurried from my desk to the studio door and having tapped lightly on it, I went inside, wondering what I might find there; what sort of man the artist would be; what he would say to me and expect of me.

Entering the bright, high ceiling'd studio almost nervously, I found the artist there already, his brushes laid out and easel set up with a canvas already upon it, while he lay on the sofa smoking a cigarette and staring up at the skylight above his head. His face was very tanned and there were deep smile lines around his eyes and mouth. He was completely bald but for a pair of heavy white brows. Yet it was a handsome face too, made more handsome by a pair of startlingly blue eyes that seemed vividly alive and full of energy despite the fact that he was gazing only up into space. He was dressed only in a pair of faded blue shorts. His body was lean and brown, with only the slightest paunch, and very strong arms. When he heard me close the door behind me, he turned to look and his eyes seemed to glitter with good humour. Then he was up and on his feet with the energy of a man at least thirty years younger.

"You must be Yasmine," he said in a voice slightly hoarse and gravelly, beaming at me and offering a large, leathery hand for me to shake. "What a pleasure. What a pleasure. You found the place? I am so glad. People get lost. Or at least that is what they tell me."

His hand was warm and dry and had a strength to it as it clasped mine that I had not expected. I thanked him, though for what I was not sure, and told him that it was a pleasure to meet him. When I did so, I called him señor and used his surname, which caused him to make a tutting sound and shake his head reprovingly.

"Call me Francis," he said. "Everyone does. Everyone I like. Only journalists and people who want things from me use my second name. And you are, of course, not one of those. Now, my dear, what can I do for you?"

"Your models have arrived," I told him.

"Have they, have they? Well, I suppose we best have them in. Time goes on of its own account, but work does not do itself."

I nodded and made to leave the room, but as I reached the door, he called after me.

"Yasmine," he said, sounding almost shy suddenly, and I turned back to face him. "Tell me, do you remember their names?"

"Maria Cristina and Maria Rosa," I told him, a little taken aback. "They said they had been here before."

"And so they have. But Maria this, Maria that, Maria I don't know. An old man cannot keep track."

"But you are not an old man," I said. The words came out almost unconsciously as I looked at his handsome face, and the moment they had I felt myself blush. However, he only smiled in return.

"I see you are as flattering and dishonest as my Violette. Well, send in the Marias and we will get to work. Do you need anything? No? If you do, just come in and ask. I banish Violette from the studio, but you are new and we cannot expect you to know everything. Besides, even a cantankerous old, or not so old, man could not be angry at being interrupted by such a charming young woman as yourself."

I smiled at that, basking in the warmth of his eyes for a moment, and then went out and told the models they could go in, and heard them giggling and the hoarse cheerful sound of the old man's voice raised in greeting as I closed the door behind them.

I spent the morning at the desk. Initially I thought there would be very little for me to do. However, I very quickly discovered that the old artist indeed received an enormous number of phone calls to be fended off and redirected to his agent. Many of the callers took my rejection with a good grace, but there were others who grew enraged and promised to ensure that bitter retribution would await me in my near future; a thing I found more amusing than upsetting. When not answering the calls, I spent my time looking at the paintings and photos that adorned the walls. They seemed to have been hung at random, without thought to the overall aesthetic of the room. Yet, all were astonishingly beautiful, varying in subject matter from the innocent to the deeply erotic. One I particularly liked showed a prostitute dressing and tucking money into her bra while a handsome old man, clearly modelled on the artist himself, lay sleeping in a large, canopied bed. I wondered, feeling a faint thrill as I did so, whether it were autobiographical; whether the painter had ever paid a girl to go to bed with him – whether he did so still and often. And for a fleeting moment, I caught myself wondering what it would be like to be paid to go to bed with him. Very different, I imagined, than it had been with my gentleman and his bartender; more tender, more romantic. He would be gentle and worshipful, I thought, concerned as much with my comfort as with his pleasure. And more grateful. He would not take for granted that I would do things for him, I thought. And as I thought that, I thought, with a vague pleasure and arousal, that I might like to give him pleasure, and to see his surprise and thankfulness as I did things for him that he did not expect. I thought how his hands would feel on my body, and how it would feel to have his strong arms clasping me tightly against him. Before I could become too wrapped up in this fantasy, however, the phone interrupted me once more and I picked it up, almost relieved by the distraction.

A couple of times the housekeeper appeared with trays of drinks and clean ashtrays and took them into the studio. She was a bustling, red-faced woman with an appearance of sternness, of authority about her that was tempered only by a hint of good humour in her dark eyes. Each time she passed through, she reminded me that if I needed anything, I should go to the kitchen and she would find it for me, and when I replied that I was fine, she gave me the look mothers often give their children when they are not taking care of themselves sufficiently. Apart for her, however, I did not see a soul the rest of the morning.

At 2 o'clock, the two models came out of the studio, smiling and giggling still, and disappeared down to what I assumed must be the kitchen. A few minutes later, the housekeeper brought out an immense tray of bread, ham, cheese, fruit and a bottle of wine and two glasses, which she placed on my desk.

"For Francis," she said, something vaguely disapproving in her tone, "and for you. He likes the secretary to lunch with him. Tell him there is fish to follow."

I picked up the tray and made to enter the studio, but she called me back.

"No, no," she said. "On the terrace, dear." Then she added in a slightly lowered tone, "And if he makes you uncomfortable, get up and leave. I have already spoken to him, but lord knows if he was listening." And then she was gone, back down to the kitchen, and I was left wondering once more.

As she had said, the artist expected me to eat lunch with him, and we did so by a glittering pool in the garden, in which a number of large, brightly coloured koi carp swam lazily between the feet of white marble statues and beds of reeds. It was a beautiful place to eat; so tranquil that it hardly seemed possible that it was in the midst of the city. There, beneath the shade of the lemon trees, with the twittering of birds and the faint plops of the carp coming up to the surface, it felt like we were in the paradise garden of a desert oasis, far from all of the world and its noise and confusion and stresses.

Throughout the meal he was a perfect gentleman and perfect companion. Yet, all the while, I could not help but wonder about the housekeeper's warning, and that of Violette. When the meal was done, however, at last I discovered what it was that they had been referring to so indirectly. Having pushed back his chair, and tossed back the last drops that remained in his wineglass, he got up and went to a sun-lounger where he slipped off his shorts modestly, with his back to me, and lay down on his stomach before turning his face to me.

"My dear girl, now you can say no, of course, and I will understand and say nothing more. And please do not be insulted. But usually, Violette is kind enough to put a little sun-cream on me so I do not burn while I sleep."

He held up the bottle with a shy, but inviting smile; a smile that none with a heart could refuse; and his voice had been a little shy, and unassuming too.

"Why not?" I thought. "After all, he is paying at least triple what anyone else would think my job was worth. And there is noting to putting sun cream on a person. It is a good thing, if anything." And so I went over to him and took the bottle and smiled and knelt by his side.

His body beneath my fingertips was smooth and surprisingly muscular. He had the legs of a swimmer, or a weightlifter, thick and strong. His back and shoulders were muscular too, the skin covering them a little hard, but silky to the touch. I took my time working the cream into him, avoiding the firm buttocks until the last moment when, with a courage that surprised me, I quickly applied a small quantity to them with a few final strokes of my hand, feeling a thrill as I did so, and then stood up.

"There," I said, "you are all done."

I suppose I expected him to thank me and close his eyes, but instead, to my surprise, he eased himself up on his elbow and rolled over, exposing himself naked before me. My eyes flickered automatically to his groin and once there, I found I could not look away. He was erect, hugely, magnificently erect, and his cock was beautiful; smooth and flawless and so perfectly proportioned that it seemed almost false. My eyes widened with astonishment as they lit upon it; astonishment, and, I have to admit, a sudden hunger. Never before had I seen such an enormous, beautiful member, so strong and thick and long.

"I will understand," I vaguely heard him say as I stared down at it, "if you are uncomfortable doing so, but Violette is in the habit of making sure I am completely covered in sun-cream, and … comfortable, before she goes on her break."

You can see how much I had changed since those long distant days with my old boyfriends, and even later with others, for then I did not hesitate, nor did any thought or worry enter my mind. I realised immediately what he was asking me to do, and I was not insulted or shocked. Staring at that cock, I had already wanted to touch it, to feel it in my hands, both of them together, to feel it swell and harden against my palms and fingers. And so I simply smiled down at him, and told him, "Of course." and squirted more cream onto my hands.

I did not immediately reach for that cock. I began with his chest and shoulders first, then I moved on to his legs, his strong calves and thighs, unable to resist the temptation to let my long hair brush lightly across his groin as I moved position. Yet, in all the time I was applying cream to other parts of his body, my eyes remained fixed on his cock watching, as it seemed to throb and grow harder, and how tiny, pearly droplets of pre-come began to glisten on its tip. I felt myself growing wet staring at it; imagining how it would feel within me, how it would fill me and it would be to feel it swell up and explode within me as I too came, my pussy gripping it, sucking in its length.

When finally I did touch it, however, taking it in my creamy hands, and gently squeezing it and rubbing up and down its immense length, it was clear that no such thing would happen. Within moments of me grasping it, his whole body seemed to tense beneath me and suddenly he came in a great fountain that sent arching jets of come over my hands and wrists and up over his stomach and chest. He lay gasping for a moment, his eyes shut and his jaw clenched, and then as the last throbs had faded, he let out a long sigh of contentment, took a wet towel from a bowl by his side that I had not seen him place there, and gave it to me to clean myself up and clean him up too.

When I was back at my desk, I felt no embarrassment or awkwardness, even when the housekeeper gave me a knowing looking when she brought me glass of lemonade later that afternoon. I understood, that was all. I understood of what Violette had warned me, and of what the housekeeper had warned me too. And I understood too, why the painter paid such high wages. Yet I did not judge him any more than I did myself. He wanted pleasure, it seemed to me, as did everyone else, and if he went about finding pleasure in an unconventional way, what did that matter? He did so with such kindness, and gentlemanliness, and after his pleasure had been taken, he was still kind and gentle, and he left me feeling happy to have given it to him, and not used or taken advantage of, or cast aside or objectified.

He asked no more of me, except that I masturbate him to a climax each day after lunch, and the rest of the time, he was kind and funny and went out of his way to make sure that I, like everyone else around me, was comfortable and happy. Each day, the ritual was repeated in exactly the same way. Each time he rolled over after I had applied sun cream to his back, I would find him as hard, and eager, and beautiful as ever; and each day his orgasm would arrive quickly and with an abundance that I had never seen in another man. Once I tasted him, licking him from my fingers when he looked away to find the towel. He was faintly sweet. But never did I touch him with any part of him but my hands. He did not ask me to, and I felt it would be taking a liberty to do so. What surprised me was that as the days went by I found myself growing almost frustrated that he never demanded any more of me. I knew that he found me attractive, and the situation erotic, from his reaction to my touch. And I would have been willing, perfectly willing, to do anything else he asked, a thing that I felt sure he must know too. I had not so much as hesitated when he wanted me to pleasure him with my hands. Why should I, were he to ask me to take him in my mouth? Or to undress and rub my naked body across his? Or even, to let him lay me down upon the sun-lounger and enter me, gently, smoothly, tantalisingly? Those thoughts, which crossed my mind whenever I was with him, caused me to grow hot and frustrated in his company. At night, having left his house, and returned to my own flat, the image of doing more, and of his hard cock, and strong arms and handsome face were what drove me to orgasm as I played with myself in the shower, or in bed between the cool sheets, yet this too seemed only to increase my frustration during the daytime; to enhance my desire for him.

On the last day I was to work for him, after we had eaten and I had applied sun cream to his back, I decided, wildly, irresponsibly and without thought to the consequences, that I was not going to look back on my time with him and feel only frustration. Thus it was that, without giving myself time to think about it, I took off my shirt, without asking his permission, and as I rubbed the sun cream into his chest and arms, I allowed my breasts to brush against his cock. He stiffened a moment, and his eyes opened wide. I merely smiled reassuringly down at him, however, and repeated the movement, this time pressing more firmly against him. I was wet then, and I no longer cared to restrain myself. The touch of him against my nipples was like the first rioter who throws stone in the midst of a protest and thereby sets of a chain of events that, the moment the stone has left his hand, are beyond his control. Making my decision, and caring nothing for the models who were then back in the studio, nor for the housekeeper in her kitchen, which looked out onto the garden, nor for anyone else who might come in, nor even for the artist himself, I rose and pressing him back against the cushions with my hands on his shoulders, I slung one leg over him and, pulling my thong aside, I eased him between the lips of my sex and slowly sank down until every inch of him was inside of me.

My god, the sensation! He felt so perfect within me, and everything else was perfect too, from the warm sun on my breasts, and the scent of sun-cream, and the lapping of the waters of the pool. Slowly at first, I rose and fell on him, but as my pleasure took over, I began, as I said before, to ride him with an almost animal fury. His look of surprise changed to one of passion, and his hands reached up to run down my back, to grasp my arse, and then to come round to squeeze and caress my breasts. His breathing became quick and deep, and over it I heard first my moans and then my screams of pleasure. A fleeting, flickering orgasm ran through me, then, as he drove in more deeply, more urgently, another, longer, more powerful, more consuming orgasm took its place, shaking me, filling me with pleasure, rumbling on and on until what seemed like an age later he grasped me against him, and

I felt his cock, that beautiful, vast cock, swell and then fill me with a torrent of sperm.

For a moment, all I could do was lie trembling upon his chest, as I felt him tremble beneath me. Yet finally, as I came back to myself, I eased myself up and dismounted him, leaned forward and kissed him lightly upon the lips, and then put on my shirt once more and walked back into the house to my desk.

The next day Violette came back from her holiday, and reluctantly I returned to what I had been doing before, but often I found myself thinking back to the artist and his garden, and wondering whether, there in the sunshine, Violette was doing what I was so happy to have had the courage to do.

# A NIGHT FOR STRANGERS

I told him that I wanted wildness, that I wanted danger, that I wanted, that I dreamed of, fantasised about, being used; that sometimes when I was alone at night, I imagined being sold by him to another man, or many men; that I imagined him giving me to his friends to use as they would, or being given by him to a stranger in payment of a debt. "Yet," I remember telling him, "you would never have the courage to do any of those things. No, it is not an insult. It is just not who you are."

I had no fear of telling him those things because I had been growing tired of him for some time then. He annoyed me and often inspired contempt in me. Possibly because he never ceased to criticise me – one of the few defects we all find unpardonable in others. Possibly because he was so sure of himself; so convinced that everything he did, and wanted, and thought was right. Yet, I had stayed with him because he was astonishingly attractive at the same time, dark and muscular with a deep tan and a self-confident egoism that I found amusing. I had met him when I was in black, reckless mood that had been with me for months, ever since a man I truly liked had left me to go back to his country. I had not cared then who I was with, so long as I did not go to bed alone. That mood, however, had begun to lift, and I knew our time together was drawing to a close.

"Would I not do those things, you think?" he challenged me, his tone of voice seeming as though he wanted to sell me there and then to anyone who would take me off my hands.

"You wouldn't dare," I said. "It would make you feel bad, or jealous, or insulted."

I had begun to tell him those things not because I expected him to want to go through with them, but simply to annoy him. However, something in his attitude caused the half-hopeful, half-anxiety-provoking thought that maybe, just maybe, he would be so annoyed with me that he would actually dare to try to fulfil at least some part of the fantasies I described to him crossed my mind. Perhaps he had begun to grow tired of me too, and saw it as a debauched way of getting rid of me, I do not know.

"Why talk of me?" he asked with a slightly scornful look darkening his handsome face. "I doubt you would do any of those things yourself, not willingly."

"Would I not?"

My words sounded full of decision, yet beneath them I felt uncertainty. I had lived out many fantasies by that point, and had thrilled in them, had found dark and previously unimagined pleasures. Yet I wondered if the idea of having myself given away like some object of desire alone, would not be a thing that would better remain as a fantasy only. At the same time that this thought occurred to me, however, I felt a defiance welling up in me to augment my desire. I did not want him to be right in his assumptions about my character. A part of me too wanted to test his arrogant, self-satisfaction; to shake the veneer of being incapable either of jealousy or shock.

"I cannot imagine it," he said, with a shrug. "They are fantasies, nothing more. Everyone has fantasies, yet only the very few dare to live them out."

"Would you care to wager that I am not one of those few?"

So that was how he found himself on a warm spring evening, sitting on a stone bench, smoking a cigarette and looking at me kneeling in the grass, my hands tied together and raised above my head by a length of velvet rope slung over the branch of a horse-chestnut tree; my clothes stripped from my body and piled nearby, waiting for someone, a stranger, to pass. As he had undressed me and bound my hands, I felt that my eyes must have appeared to be burning with a bright light of passion; a light more intense than he had ever caused to burn in them. My body, when his fingers grazed over it in taking off my clothes, was responsive and eager, and when he peeled off my underwear, I could feel the heat coming from between my legs in waves. What he felt, I do not know; a strange mixture of feelings; arousal, coupled with contempt, jealousy, bitterness, desire, perhaps. I think we both knew that this was the end of what lay between us. Yet did he *want* to watch the way it ended? Or did stubbornness and pride hold him there? Or perhaps a sense of duty? We had agreed a safety word, and a safety sign in case I could not speak. And we had agreed that he would intervene with whatever force required if I wanted saving. But we had agreed nothing else; no boundaries, no restrictions, and most of all we had made no promises of what the future would hold after the experience was done. I do not think he cared any more about the future than I did. Yet perhaps he did, after all, want that experience. For my part, I felt a more powerful conviction than ever that I wanted it to be him who was there with me, watching me revel in it, and knowing that in all probability after it was done, he would never see me again, or that if he did, it would never be in the same way. I wanted to catch glimpses of his face as whatever happened happened and see what emotions would appear in those green eyes that normally glittered with such a devil-may-care, self-satisfied gleam. Even then, however, as I delighted in this vicious pleasure, I realised that, strangely, I trusted in him absolutely to protect me; trusted that he would not let anything happen to me that I did not want to happen. I was sure of that as I looked at him while I knelt naked and vulnerable in so public a place. I realise now, how strange that is; how strange indeed relationships between people, and people themselves, are. Often we may have trust in those we loathe, whilst distrusting those we love.

After a time, a couple passed by walking along the path that ran close to the tree, and the bench where he sat. The man stopped in his tracks, seemingly unconscious that he had done so, and stood for a moment staring hungrily at me. The woman, however, quickly took his arm and dragged him forcefully onwards hissing something sharply at him and glancing in my lover's direction with disgust in her dark eyes. He watched them go, then looked at me kneeling still on the grass. I hoped that nothing about me spoke of shame or embarrassment, since I felt quite the opposite. The moment had given me a dark pleasure. I hoped that instead of shame, he saw a kind of wild smile on my lips, and that my eyes seemed eager. I hoped too that my obvious excitement would infect him, sending a dark thrill through him too that he had never felt before nor would again. I realised then that the apathy I had felt toward him, the contempt, had all disappeared – to be replaced by a desire for him to enjoy my fantasy as it was fulfilled.

After the couple, an old man passed slowly by going down the hill. He looked at me and paused for a moment, smiling leeringly. He did not stop for long either, however, but having run his eyes all over my body, started off on his way again, merely shooting my lover a wink and a look that struck me as one of lecherous approval.

I let out a sigh of relief when he was gone. All the time his eyes had been on me, I had been shifting uncomfortably in my restraints, feeling a blush of colour rising in my cheeks. That old man had not been part of my fantasy, and I was sure that had he approached me, touched me, made to take me, I would have called out for my lover to stop it, and perhaps that would have been the end of it. Perhaps, in that moment, after the old man was gone, I had even been considering calling it off; wondering whether in fact reality could ever match what I had imagined, or whether it could only be something sordid and degrading and not erotic at all. I said nothing, however, and a few minutes later I was glad of it as two men in their thirties, of a very different stamp, came into sight along the path. One was blond, the other dark, yet both handsome and elegantly dressed. The dark one frowned, but the blond smiled broadly and spoke to my lover in English.

"What have we here?" he asked, his voice deep and languid. "May I?"

My lover shrugged and waved a hand in my direction.

"Go ahead," he told the men and then, catching the dark one's expression darken further, he added; "That's what she wants."

The blond approached me, and walked slowly around me, examining me with a hungry, wicked smile. I could almost feel the hard caress of his eyes upon me. My heart was racing, but I felt myself straighten unconsciously, thrusting my breasts forward and my arse out, my knees shifting a little in the grass to allow my legs to open.

"Aren't you a beauty," he told me, shaking his head wonderingly. Then he whistled through his teeth. "And my God, you are built like something out of a fucking dream."

He reached down then and cupped my breasts, squeezing them together before leaning down to lick and kiss first one nipple then the other. The intensity of the sensation seemed amplified by the situation, and yet it was almost an unreal sensation at the same time; a sensation such as one feels when someone touches one in a dream; a sensation that at once doe not exists, and yet is felt not only in the part of one being touched, but seems to ripple through the whole of one's being; mind and body alike.

"You don't mind, do you?" he asked, rising once more a minute or two later. I thought for a moment the questions was directed at me, then I realised that it had been for his friend who was standing then beside the bench on which my lover sat.

"As you wish," the friend said, with a shrug of his shoulders, and the blond smiled and undid his flies and took out a half-hard cock and held it close to my face.

"What do you think of that, gorgeous? Want to make me happy?"

I had wondered, while he had walked around me, how I would react in that moment in which the worlds of fantasy and reality finally met. Perhaps, I had thought, I would, after all, give the safety word indicating that I had changed my mind and wanted to be rescued from my own dark dreams. I almost expected to hear the word come from me then, in response to his question. Yet the reply that did come from me was a very different one. Not one word escaped me, but immediately I felt myself lean forward on my restraints and then I had taken his smooth, thick cock between my lips with an almost desperate urgency. I consumed him, buried him in my mouth until my nose was pressed against his flat, hard stomach and my eyes were watering. I sucked wildly, pulling my mouth from him with a squelching pop and letting his cock rest against my face as I drew breath, only to dive forward once more and swallow every inch of it in one smooth movement. The blond meanwhile seemed transported. His wicked, hungry smile had disappeared; replaced by a look of astonishment and bliss. Yet I hardly saw him as a person capable of feeling, of sensation. He was a blur above me, a beautiful body, with a perfectly formed member that slipped so silken smooth over my tongue and filled my mouth so exquisitely. I became so enraptured by what I was doing, by the eroticism of the situation and the unknown nature of the man whom I pleasured so fervently, that I forgot even to look at my lover. How he reacted, what look appeared on his face and in his bright green eyes, I do not know and cannot guess. As far as I was concerned, he had for that moment disappeared from my world.

When I had been going for some time without ever ceasing or slowing, growing only hungrier, more lascivious with every passing minute, the dark one apparently gave in to temptation also, tossed the cigarette he had been smoking into the dust, and came up behind me. The first I knew of it was a sharp, stinging pain as he slapped my arse, a firm, ringing slap, and in a commanding voice said; "Up!"

Without even understanding what had happened, my body responded immediately, and I found myself rising from my knees to my feet but without ever letting the blond's cock slip from my mouth, so that I stood bent over at the waist, offering myself to the dark one with a willingness that I seemed to have no control over. It was as if I were no longer the mistress of myself; as if all control, all decision-making had been taken over by my body and the power of my desire; the power of the fantasy I was enacting. The dark one meanwhile responded to my movement by bending forward and burying his tongue in the folds of my pussy, for a minute or so, no longer, causing a mini-orgasm to surge through me almost at the first caress. Then he rose and undid his trousers. His cock, like him, was dark and thick, and he rubbed it teasingly over my pussy for a moment before, abruptly, in one smooth, effortless movement, which showed how wet I was, he buried it in me to the hilt. I heard myself moan and felt myself begin to slam my buttocks back against him, forcing him as deep as he would go inside of me, while all the while continuing my lavish attentions on the man in front of me. The sensation of having the two of them inside me at the same time, was unlike any I had ever felt before. To be at once totally in their power, and yet at the same time all powerful over them; to have them, unconsciously almost, pleasuring me, and to hold the key to their pleasure in my mouth and pussy; to be able to take it away simply by jerking my lips from the blond one and calling out the safety word; it felt intoxicatingly powerful. And then there was the feeling too of being filled, so absolutely and completely that my mouth and sex seemed almost connected to one another. Combined, the two feelings took the mini-orgasm that the dark one's tongue had given me increased it twenty fold and sent it flooding through me again and again. I came and came and came again, yet it went on, the dark man fucking me slowly to begin with,

with those long, confident strokes, but gradually increasing his rhythm until he was slamming into me, forcing me forward on my restraints to bury the blond's cock deeper and deeper in my mouth. My moans turned to stifled cries, and my body began to shake as my bound hands clawed desperately at the dark one's stomach, urging him on. At one point my legs gave way, but the dark man caught me about the hips and lifted me and went on fucking me until both he and the blond came together, filling my mouth and sex simultaneously with their come. When finally they withdrew their cocks and did up their trousers, they left me hanging forward on my restraints, gasping for breath, my legs no longer capable of supporting me, my whole body shaking with passion and fulfilled desire.

    I was drained; barely aware. Yet I wanted more. And I got it. I became conscious that a group of boys in their late teens or early twenties had stopped beside my lover and had been looking on for some time exchanging bawdy comments, laughing, whooping. For all their words and jokes, they seemed nervous of approaching while the two older men were with me, but as the men walked down the hill, they seemed to find their courage and moved forward and formed a circle around me, just as the men in my neighbour's flat had formed around her. I looked up, thrilling at the dirty sexiness of the scene and I think, though still I hung limp, as though all the energy had been drained from me by the pleasure the dark man had brought me, I must have smiled. Quickly, hands grasped my breasts and arse and pussy, some unskilled, some not, but all exciting, and the touch of those hands seemed to breathe some life into me again, and I began wriggling against them, revelling in the attention, revelling in the groping caresses; the anticipation of what was to come. My reaction in turn seemed to spur the boys on, and any restraint they might have felt seemed to disappear into the dusk. Trousers were hurriedly unbuttoned and cocks drawn out. Fingers slipped into my sperm-drenched sex and toyed across my anus. And once more waves of pleasure began to flow over me and through me again; the pleasure of the touches, of the lasciviousness of the situation and over all with the knowledge that my lover sat not five yards away, watching it all unfold.

These youngsters were rougher with me than the other two had been, but even that I revelled in. Cocks were slapped against my tongue and cheeks. My erect nipples were twisted and pinched. They fucked my mouth. They fucked my pussy wildly, taking it in turns, seeming to lack neither energy or stamina. When one came quickly, filling my pussy, gasping and moaning, his orgasm was received a howl of jeers from his companions, and he was quickly pushed aside. I did not care, however. I felt like a wild thing then, utterly reduced to only the sensations of lust and pleasure. My mouth flew from cock to cock while I thrust back almost violently onto whichever of them was inside me. My vision was reduced to a blur, yet my sense of touch, of feeling, was heightened to a barely comprehendable intensity. Every thrust, every touch and pinch, every tongue that caressed me, every set of lips that kissed me, seemed to raise the level of my now almost constant orgasm. My moans, even stifled as they were by the cock in my mouth, must have been loud enough to echo through the trees. And all I did only drove the boys on harder. One, bolder than the others, when his turn came, scooped the sperm from my sex and used it to lubricate my anus, then drove himself mercilessly inside me. For a split second, I felt a sweet, sharp pain, then a new pleasure swept through me. Breaking free from the cock in my mouth and I let out a half-moan, half-scream of pleasure as the most powerful orgasm of all roared through me. Yet still I wanted only more. When the boy in my arse came, I thrust wildly back against him and at the same moment another came in my mouth and I swallowed his sperm down half-in-shock and half with delight. I swallowed his sperm and went on sucking the next cock that was thrust between my lips with the same eagerness. Another cock entered my arse and again I tore myself from the boy in front of me and let out a long, wild cry of ecstasy, but this time the cock was immediately thrust back in my mouth, muffling the cry and I went back to sucking at it as though demented. For five minutes, five hours, five lifetimes, I went on sucking and shaking and coming and thrusting back against whoever was fucking me, and then when the last had finished, pulling out to send arching jets of come shooting over my back, I fell limp once more in my restraints, blinded by pleasure, my hair plastered over my face, my body shuddering with aftershocks of wanton bliss.

When I came back to myself, the faces of the boys swam back into view, all handsome and dazed and unbelieving. They exchanged looks as they dressed themselves, but no words. Several glanced at my lover and then looked away as if uncertain whether to feel pride or shame. Only once they had gone, disappearing down the path toward the city, did I hear their voices once more, their whooping cries and shouts of laughter.

No-one else was in sight then, and I wondered whether it were all over, but then my lover stepped forward himself to take me. He fucked me, slipping in easily on the sperm inside me and my hotness, and my sex seemed to suck him in and hold him, and I felt a last, weaker orgasm run through me and heard myself cry out, and then he came at last, mingling his spendings with those of the others.

He untied my wrists roughly when he was done and left me there on my knees, and walked slowly away through the dusk. He wanted no more it, I knew even then. Myself, I collapsed onto the grass and lay there, destroyed by ecstasy. Yet for me, I knew even then that I would want the experience repeated, surpassed even. How it could be surpassed I was not sure. But such things can always be surpassed for those willing to brave the tantalising, all-embracing darkness.

As a way of ending a relationship, to me it did not seem unpoetic, and I was happy the relationship that had existed between us came to an end there with that last, wild, debauched memory. However, already, I was thinking, as my mind began to work once more, what adventures still lay before me; what pleasures awaited all those who had the courage to open themselves up to them.

# EPILOGUE

"I have read your notebook ten times, yet still I do not know which of the stories are true and which are merely fantasy," Dominic told me, the first time we saw one another after the original exchange of notebooks. He seemed nervous, pacing about the room with an unlit cigarette in one hand, that he kept putting between his lips as if to light and then taking out again. "I think that perhaps everything you wrote is true or at least that there was an element of truth in everything you wrote. And thinking that, makes me feel something I did not expect to feel."

"What does it make you feel?" I asked, not wanting either to confirm his suspicions or to deny them, and realising at that moment that if he reacted that way it meant that much of what he had written could not have been true. That disappointed me. Everything I had written had been true. He looked at me for a moment or two, his brows creased and handsome face thoughtful. Then he smiled. It was a smile that seemed to seek to contain all of his old carelessness, yet beneath that was somehow different from the smile I had so often seen before we had read one another's stories; tinged perhaps with unhappiness or concern.

"It is not, you understand, only in what you have done, or imagined doing; but in how you describe it, in what you drew from it, what you felt about it. In truth, I feel having read your stories that I am not *enough* for you," he said finally. "Not imaginative enough; not experimental enough; not libertine enough. It is funny. I never thought before that any woman could truly be beyond me in those things; be more passionate, more courageous, to have desires that ran deeper and were more coloured by danger than my own. It just goes to show how little we know of ourselves, I suppose."

"Yes," I said, feeling a little sad and concerned too as I looked at him, though for him rather than for myself. "Knowing oneself is the hardest thing of all – knowing, that is, and accepting."

He had stopped pacing by then, and came over to me and knelt at my feet where I sat on the bed.

"And you?" he asked. "How do you feel, having read my stories and knowing what was contained in your own?"

With those beautiful eyes fixed on mine, I could not bring myself to lie to him. Nor, would there have been any reason to do so but cowardice. Lying to him then, as with all lies, would only have spared him suffering temporarily in order to inflict greater suffering were the truth to become known.

"I think," I said, gently, yet I hoped, neither patronisingly nor pityingly, "that perhaps I *am* a little too much for you. Or at least that I would be in the future. Too much, though still less so than many men I have known."

He sighed and slowly nodded his head as though he had known what my response would be before ever I had uttered it.

"And so?" he asked.

"And so…"

"What happens now?"

I smiled down at him, and taking his hands in mine drew him up beside me onto the crisp white coverlet.

"Now, we each have a collection of stories to keep ourselves amused," I told him. "And whatever we have learned from them, whether we like it or not, we are lucky. We, unlike most people, have had the opportunity to catch a true glimpse something of the imagination of one another; the imagination and the history. How many people have that chance? How many people truly know anything of either their lover's true history or their desires? Truly know, I mean, not merely suspect."

"Almost none, I suppose," he said.

"So there you have it," I went on. "Almost none. And tell me, having read what I wrote, do you still desire me?"

"More than ever," he said, a faint gleam igniting in his eyes. "I want you now in ways that I never knew I wanted you before."

"Well then," I said, "whether or not I am too much for you, don't let's worry about that tonight. Tonight, at least, we can make one last story to add to the others." And I leaned over as I said that and kissed him and as I kissed him, I felt something stir within me, as though a passionate new chapter of my life were about to begin, the nature of which was as yet a mystery to me. The process of writing my stories and of reading his, had recalled to me who I truly am, who I wanted to be; of the mystery and adventure and passion that the world still held. I realised that at some point I had begun once more to hide that person, from the world and from myself, and that was something I did not wish to do. Thus, I publish the stories as they are, to prevent me one day burning them and there after forgetting them. The stories of Dominic, I returned to him before we parted. Though I kept copies of them for my own pleasure, it would not have been fair to publish them here. Perhaps, however, if he reads this book, he may reach out to me, and if he does, perhaps he could be convinced to publish his own also.

Printed in Great Britain
by Amazon